Cry for a Shadow

CHRYS PAUL FLETCHER

Cry for a Shadow

G. P. PUTNAM'S SONS, *New York*

To Violet Turner

"Math and aftermath, wait outside the hall
 And fall
          —where emperors stood."

Contents

Cry for a Shadow

1. / *Math*

THE gray-white cigarette smoke rose in a lazy cloud, spiraling across the whole room.

The room was a dressing room, small, white-painted and untidy.

Spud sat in the middle, organizing; Chris Plater sat on the table; Lorraine sat on the floor, and the journalist sat in a chair.

"Well, I don't think we can say any more than that. It's almost nine o'clock now. You don't mind—?"

Spud hustled the journalist to the door.

"And I hope we can see you for that drink afterward."

Spud shut the door. He turned to Chris. "I'll go and see everything's ready. It shouldn't be long now. The bloke said he'd tell you five minutes before you go on."

"Yeah, okay, Spud."

Spud went out and closed the door.

Chris laughed.

"What's up with you?"

"Oh, I feel mad. Like I was high or something. I don't know. Let's go out and find a party after this."

"We can't. We don't even know anyone around here."

"We can find someone. Or we could go down to Brighton for tonight. It ain't far. What about that?"

Lorraine held up her hand to him and pulled him down on the floor. "I know where I wanna go," she said.

"Where's that?"

They grinned because they both knew where it was, but he just wanted her to say it.

"Bed."

He shrugged and pulled himself down toward her until their faces were almost touching. "If we went down to Brighton, we could sleep out on the beach. Under the pier." He kissed her and ran his hand through her hair.

He felt a great feeling of excitement within him, almost as if he could reach out for the stars. He'd felt it ever since they arrived. A marvelous feeling of power, as if he needed to do something, go to a party or talk or argue or make love all night long.

He could feel the tense, dance-hall atmosphere all around him. The noise of the records being played outside. The hubbub of chatter. The brightness of all the lights.

It was like the sudden excitement he used to feel a couple of years ago, when he was seventeen and before he became known, when he used to go off for all those mad weekends with Tom and his cousin and half a dozen girls. When they used to stand on the beach at Clacton or somewhere and toss a coin to see who would sleep with who, or where they'd go to the next day.

Or it was like those feelings he got sometimes when he was singing, sudden moments of intensity which came to him out of the blue, when he felt everything so strongly that he just wanted to burst.

Or perhaps it was like those moments of depression he got, when the whole world just seemed ridiculous and impossible, and the little trivialities came crashing in on him like some great suffocating canvas bag, and all he could do was to lie there on his bed, tortured and futile.

The knock came on the door.

"They'll be ready for you in a minute."

"All right."

He stood up and pulled Lorraine up after him. "I'd better go. You coming out?"

"I'll come and stand at the side."

He put his hands around her waist, ran them down over the tight blue of her jeans. She pushed her fingers inside his shirt and down across his chest.

They kissed for a moment, the face and the neck. Chris picked up his cigarettes, and they moved out of the room and down the passage toward the stage. He lit a cigarette as they walked toward the small stage. Behind the drawn curtains the stage was empty, apart from a single table and, on top of it, a glass of water.

Spud came in with Chris' guitar, and they stood there in the middle of the stage for a moment, fitting Chris' mouth organ into the rest on top of the guitar.

"How many people out there?"

"Six or seven hundred. How you feeling?"

"Great. We were talking about going to Brighton afterward. How d'you feel about it?"

"I dunno. I think perhaps you oughta get some sleep." Spud looked concerned. His mind was going back over the periods of depression Chris got. Life was like a continual tightrope of elation and depression. Lately Chris had felt frustrated, depressed. Spud didn't know what to do. One minute Chris was on top of the world, the next minute he talked as if he were trying to die.

He shrugged his shoulders and looked first at Chris and then at Lorraine. "What were ya gonna do down in Brighton, anyway?"

"Oh, I dunno. You find yourself a bird, and we'll all go down and buy some wine and have a party out on the beach."

Spud brushed his hand over his thin semblance of a moustache. His long hair hung down across the sides of his face, reaching almost to his shoulders, the typical hippie. Finally he gave in. He smiled.

"Oh, all right then," he said. "I'll go out later on and try to get some wine. You'd better get yourself ready. The curtain'll be going up in a minute."

"Yeah, sure."

Chris put the strap of the guitar over his shoulder and listened to the noise of the record just finishing outside. "Try and find me some more water, can ya, Spud?"

"Yeah, I'll get you another couple of glasses."

Spud disappeared again to the side of the stage. The dancehall manager appeared and nodded a couple of times to Spud. Finally the record finished, and everything was quiet for a few seconds. Someone made gestures on each side of the stage, and the curtains began to open. There were noises from the crowds in front of the stage. Chris and Lorraine stood talking for a moment in the middle of the stage, and then they both laughed at something, and Lorraine moved off to the side, out of sight.

Chris walked forward to the microphone at the front of the stage. Just in front of him and to each side there stood a line of bouncers to control the crowd, and just beyond the bouncers stood a girl in a green jumper, smoking and talking to her friend.

Chris plucked a couple of times at the strings of the

guitar, holding the cigarette still in his right hand. The tune of the song became gradually more clear. He moved nearer to the microphone. "Hey, Mr. Tambourine Man . . ."

The girl in green pressed herself nearer toward the stage. On the outskirts of the dance floor a few people danced. Lorraine stood talking to someone, out of sight at the edge of the stage. Her hair was long, straight and light brown. She wore a leather jacket slung loosely over her shoulders and a blue shirt tucked into her jeans.

Chris glanced over at her. The cigarette ash fell from his right hand and landed at his feet. He picked at the guitar strings with his thumb and held the cigarette between his first and second fingers. The sound of the guitar blasted out alone over the two loudspeakers. There was no accompaniment to it at all. At the break between verses, Chris brought his mouth down onto the mouth organ, and the crowd swayed to the distorted sounds from the loudspeaker.

Chris half-closed his eyes in semiagony. It was impossible to explain the meaning "Mr. Tambourine Man" had for him. There was a quote from Donovan Leitch on it: "People who say they dig Dylan don't really understand. If they really understood, it'd be painful to listen to."

He raised his head in the air, glanced at the ceiling. Dim yellow and red colors seemed to float above his head from the lights on the ceiling. The words came from his mouth automatically, the recited words of the prophet. He finished the song, drew on the cigarette, and then threw it away.

After the next song he turned around behind him, pulled the table up nearer to the microphone and took a sip of the water. The water was not there for effect but because he needed it. It was an idiosyncrasy of his. He was hardly ever without a drink of water beside him all day long.

He moved forward again to the microphone. "This is something I wrote about nine months ago over in Spain." He strummed his fingers over the strings of the guitar. "It's called 'Toledo Dream.' "

There was a burst of cheers at the name of the song. Chris could see Spud moving out among the crowd in the direction of the refreshment bar. Spud waved at him, and he waved back, laughing. Spud bought some bottles of Coke and made his way back, around the edge of the dance floor. He reached the stage again and stood with Lorraine.

"How's he feeling?"

"Great. Why?"

"I dunno. Sometimes he worries me. He's been getting too depressed, too extreme."

"Christ, you sound like you're his mother or something."

He laughed. "I am, man, I am."

The song finished, and Spud went onto the stage with a couple of the bottles of Coke.

"Couldn't find any water, so I got some Coke instead."

"Thanks." Chris took a drink from one of the bottles and put it down onto the table.

The evening wore on noisily. Chris lit another cigarette and drank the two bottles of Coca-Cola and the rest of the water. After his sixth song, he sat down on the edge of the stage and played from there. The girl in the green jumper pushed through the line of bouncers to stand at his side. She offered him a cigarette, lit it for him and held it up in front of his face. He took it gratefully and played some Bob Dylan tune on his guitar while he smoked.

Spud moved out onto the dance floor again and sat down at a table by the refreshment bar opposite a couple of girls. They talked for a while about Chris and pop music. One of the girls nodded toward the stage. "How'd you meet him, anyway?"

"I met him in London. Some coffee bar. It was about nineteen months ago. He'd been in trouble with the police, and it was just before he made his first record. He was sitting there with his bird, Lorraine, writing. They were talking about sex, and I just got drawn into the conversation. I dunno how, man. I was stoned, anyway."

"Why d'they call you Spud? What's your real name?"

"I haven't got a real name. Least, I never tell it to people."

"Doesn't even Chris know it?"

"He's never asked me."

They sat smoking for a few minutes. The lights dimmed, revolving in a slow rainbow of reds and greens. From the loudspeakers the sound of the guitar came out louder than ever. Spud said, "You feel like coming down to Brighton tonight? We're going down in the van—me, Chris and Lorraine. Chris wants to get some wine, have a party on the beach. He's feeling real insane tonight. He needs to get drunk and fall asleep out on the cold sand. It'll do him good."

"When're you coming back?"

"Who knows? We haven't gotta be anywhere over the weekend. I s'pose we can leave Brighton sometime on Monday. Tuesday, perhaps."

Chris paused for a moment before the microphone. He'd almost finished now. He felt good still, fresh, but his time was almost over. He said, "This is the last song. It was written in Soho, sometime last year. It's called 'Cry for a Shadow.'"

Somewhere a girl screamed. Someone broke through to the stage and kissed him just as he started to play. "Cry for a Shadow" was the weirdest song Chris had ever written. There was no singing in it at all. It was

21

merely a poem spoken against the sound of the guitar. It was a poem to a hippie called July-Anne, whom he'd met on Folkestone beach three years ago, when he was sixteen and she was almost twenty.

He smiled to himself as he spoke the poem. The words stirred the memories inside him of being free, the memories of sleeping out for the night on some deserted beach, being able to do what he liked, being free. He thought about Brighton, about the night ahead of him. They could drive down madly in the van, sit in the back with the radio blaring and someone strumming on the guitar, stop at some all-night café for something to eat, and then carry on blindly until they reached Brighton.

He tossed back his head, looked to where Spud was sitting at the back of the crowd. His long hair cascaded over his face, covered his eyes. He blew the hair away and looked down again to the girl in green. She smiled. He closed his eyes again and concentrated.

At the end of the song there was a mad clamoring for the stage. Chris moved back behind the descending curtains. He ran over to Lorraine, took her back with him to the dressing room.

"They don't lock up yet at this place, do they?"

"Not yet. They play a few more records."

They closed the dressing-room door.

"Come on, get yourself undressed. I been thinking

about making love to you for the last three quarters of an hour."

They pulled each other to the floor on the far side of the table. There was breathing and active semisilence. The clothes came off them quickly. There was little speaking, no kissing; they merely moved themselves slowly against each other's bodies. Lorraine pulled Chris quickly on top of her. He pushed himself between her legs, straightened himself for a minute, entering the void.

The sex was like an explosion. Moving. Groping. Pressing. Feeling. A buildup of the senses. The legs pressed tight together. The bodies. A glance downward at the interlocked limbs. The sight of skin moving against skin. The taste of salt in the mouth. The smells of the warm bodies.

They finished, and the climax oozed slowly from between their legs and onto the floor. They stood up, lit cigarettes and stood there, naked and smoking.

Spud walked along the passage with the two girls. They opened the door and came in. Spud said, "This is Kathy, Pat."

Lorraine turned to them and said, "Hi." No one was worried about Chris and Lorraine being naked. Spud came and got a cigarette.

"Pat and Kathy are coming to Brighton with us. We went out about half an hour ago and got a few bottles of wine. We've got some marijuana too—only enough for about three of us, but Pat and Kathy don't want any, so it's all right."

Chris found himself some water and got dressed while Lorraine put back on her jeans. Chris stood drinking water and talking about the van.

"You ready to go?"

"Sure. Let's get going."

II

Chris was nineteen years old. He was folk singer, hippie, mod and rocker. When he was seventeen, there had been a fight with a policeman on Clacton beach. Chris had been there somewhere in the middle of the fight. When everyone had been caught, Chris was accused of the policeman's murder.

Three weeks after the trial, he had made his first record.

That was all there was to it. He had met Lorraine about eighteen hours before the policeman's death. They had hidden in a deserted beach hut together while the police were searching for them. They had been sleeping together on and off ever since.

There was a jolt in the back of the van as they drove over a bump in the road. Spud sat in the front, driving. Pat sat next to him, and the others sat in the back. The van was old and filthy. On the side of it there were names scrawled in lipstick, messages written in the dust. One of the two back windows was broken, the other one smeared in dirt.

Chris handed over the bottle of wine. Kathy drank from it, handed it to Lorraine.

"Some American film star's just got married. I heard it on the news. He's been divorced four times already. And he's only twenty-six years old."

"Best of luck to him. He must be mad."

"Sex mad, most likely."

"I don't see what you have to get married for just to have sex. You can get that anywhere."

"Yeah, but it's more comfortable when you can do it in your own bed, without having to get rid of the girl before your parents come around the next morning."

"How do you know his parents go around to see him the next morning?"

Pat laughed. "They always do. When I'm with a boy, they do, anyway."

"You'd better marry him, then," Kathy said.

"I don't believe in it. Marriage is just a small piece of paper, a tax rebate and a few pieces of confetti."

Chris laughed. "That's bloody marvelous. You oughta write that down. You don't really believe in marriage, though, do ya?" he said to Kathy.

"Yeah, I s'pose so. Why not? You don't have to marry the first girl you ever sleep with or anything like that, but when you really get serious about someone, I don't see why you shouldn't marry her."

"But you can live the rest of your life with someone without marrying them. Marriage is just a license for sex. You don't need a license to make you feel respectable when you go to bed with someone, do you?"

"Oh, I don't know. You're confusing me. Don't you think if you decide to live with someone, then marriage makes it all more final, so that the other person knows you're always gonna stay with her and not just walk out as soon as you find someone else?"

Lorraine said, "Yeah, of course it makes it final, but who wants to marry a boy just so that he'll be tied to her when she gets old? If Chris sleeps with some girl he picks up after a concert or someone he meets in a coffee bar, then what's wrong with that? I don't care about it. And he wouldn't care if I went to bed with some other boy. He knows that going to bed with someone else would never mean as much to me as going to bed with him. And if it ever did mean more with someone else, then I'd stop living with Chris and go and live with the other boy. It's as simple as that. We don't wanna get married to each other because it'd make a mockery of everything we believe in. And it makes a mockery of most other people's beliefs, too, otherwise there wouldn't be so many divorces."

Kathy lit herself a cigarette and finally smiled. She said, "By the looks of him, he'll be sleeping with all three of us tonight. And probably a few more besides."

There was a laugh from Chris. He took a swig of the

wine and said, "I wanna get drunk and go for a mid-night swim before we do anything else."

"Yeah, we can go for a swim and then have a naked orgy out on the beach."

"And then smoke those reefers Spud's got, and not go to sleep all night."

They chattered and laughed on for almost forty minutes. The van rocked backward and forward over the uneven road, and they stopped eventually at an all-night roadhouse thirty miles from Brighton. Lorraine jumped down from the back of the van, a bottle of red wine in her hand. She drained the last remaining dregs of wine from the bottle and then threw it away into the bushes at the back of the car park. Chris ran to the door of the café, and they crowded inside. A crowd of rockers pushed past them, moving over to the jukebox. A pair of girls stood by a window, looking out at the road.

They moved to the counter and bought something to eat. Egg and chips, fish and chips, sausage.

Chris and Spud bought something to drink and carried it over to the table. They sat for a while, talking madly. The crowd of rockers stood by the jukebox still. One of them looked over at Chris and mentioned his name to the girl at his side. The girl shook her head.

"It can't be."

"Well, I don't know. It looks like him."

"Yeah, it does."

Lorraine ate her fish and chips. She thought back to the time when there had been the fight with the policeman on Clacton beach. They had eaten out of roadhouse cafés then, too. For five days they'd hitchhiked across country, from road house to roadhouse, trying to get away from the police net which had been spread out to catch them. They'd stolen some money out of a church box and lived for five days off their wits.

She smiled at the memory of it. Spud started telling a joke. "There was this ship sailing from London out to somewhere in Africa. They were carrying a cargo of dogs, two hundred barrels of beer, and a group of monks and nuns who were going out as missionaries. So, about a hundred miles off the coast of Africa, there was a shipwreck. Everyone clung onto bits of the ship, and eventually they were all washed up onto a couple of islands. All the nuns were washed up onto one island, and all the monks were washed up onto the other one—with the dogs and the barrels of beer.

"Anyway, after about two weeks the monks had drunk all the beer, and all the beer barrels were empty. So some of the dogs started climbing into the empty barrels and floating across to the other island. All the monks stood watching this, and in the end they decided to float over to the other island, too. They got into the barrels, and after a few hours in the water they drifted across to the nuns.

"About two months later one of the nuns went up

to the mother superior, and she said, 'Mother Superior, I've got a confession to make. I'm going to have a baby.' "

Spud paused for a moment. "So the mother superior said, 'That's nothing. I'm going to have puppies.' "

They all burst into laughter and started to tell more jokes. Spud drank coffee, and the others drank Coca-Cola. After about half an hour they were ready to go again, and they crowded back into the van. At Haywards Heath they stopped to pick up a hitchhiker and to give Spud a chance to have a drink of the red wine.

Chris and the hitchhiker shook hands.

"Chris."

"Mark."

"This is Pat, Kathy, Lorraine. That's Spud."

"Hi."

"How far you going?"

"Brighton."

"So are we."

"Great. I thought I'd have to spend the night some-where around here. I been thumbing for five hours."

"Christ, where'd you start out?"

"London. A friend of mine's down in Brighton, and I gotta see him."

Mark settled down with his back against the wall. He was twenty, wore long hair and an olive-green parka. He wore black corduroy trousers stained with splashes of paint and traces of mud. Someone offered him the wine bottle, and he drank from it gratefully. He'd seen Chris' name written on the side of the van when he first climbed in. He said, "You're Chris Plater?"

"Yeah."

"I got a twin sister. She met you once at a party."

"What's her name?"

"Mary M—"

"Whereabouts was the party?"

"Cornwall. St. Ives."

"I remember something about it. Last September. She wasn't the one with the craze about Dostoevsky?"

Mark nodded. "Yeah, that's her."

They grinned, chatted, drank and smoke. Chris felt as if he could never be tired again in his life. He'd been listening, drinking, talking, since six o'clock that morning. Or perhaps it was past midnight already, perhaps it was since yesterday morning. He didn't know, didn't care. Everything seemed mad, marvelous. It was as if he were seeing everything through the haze of half-smoked cannabis or the blur of LSD. He leaned forward over Pat's shoulder and opened the window. The cold air rushed past his face, blew through his uncombed hair. He drew deep breaths of it, gulping. The wine came around to him again, and he drank from it quickly. It was as if he were drinking the wine for the very first time, as if before he'd never even tasted it.

He threw back his head; trickles of the wine ran

warmly down over his shirt, over his chest. Lorraine drew herself over to him, and they fell to the floor, kissing, in the moving van.

"Whereabouts is this friend of yours staying down in Brighton?"

"I'm not sure. I won't start looking for him till some-time tomorrow morning. He knows I'm coming. He'll find me." Mark took out cigarettes and offered them around.

He smoked for a while and talked to Kathy. The van rolled on along the near-deserted roads. Spud drove at a steady fifty, turning his eyes from the road every so often to talk or laugh with Pat. Mark lay with his arm around Kathy, his back pushed up hard against the vibrating wall of the van.

They reached a merry-go-round. Another ten miles to go. Chris and Lorraine talked, voices low. Eventually there was laughter.

"I can't play that one. I don't know the words."

"Well, play something else, then."

Spud half turned toward the back of the van. "Yeah, play something. Play some Bob Dylan."

"What d'you want?"

"I don't know. 'Blowing in the Wind.' "

Pat passed Chris the guitar. He started to play Bob Dylan's "Blowing in the Wind." The others sang along with him as he played it.

Words flashed across Chris' mind. Dylan had once

said that to sing "Blowing in the Wind" was usually nothing but a waste of time because before it could mean anything to you, you first had to discover the wind. "At school I flunked out. I read a lot, but not the required readings." "I still say that some of the greatest criminals are those who turn their backs and look the other way."

"Into my writing I put only my talent, but into my life I have put my genius."

"I shall be my own epitaph, world, should you ever dare look upon me."

"I can give you nothing but blood, sweat, toil and . . ."

Chris heard the noise of a car horn screaming through the air. He looked up. Spud was swearing as they avoided a passing car. He laughed. The van careened crazily on through the darkness, over the bumps in the road.

Lorraine strummed on the guitar. Pat sang. The noises drowned everything. Everyone was talking at once, everything was happening. The quotations faded from Chris' mind. He was left with nothing but the feeling of aliveness, the feeling of excitement, the feeling that he must do something—sing, dance, argue—all night, all week long.

Lorraine collapsed on top of him again. He took hold of her, pulled her mouth over to his. They tasted the remains of red wine on each other's lips, in each other's mouths. Chris moved his hands across her body, over the slimness of her jeans. The bumping of the car. The noise. The excitement. It acted upon his brain, made him drunker, more restless, more energetic. It pulled at something inside him, the memory of the nights with his cousin years ago at Folkestone, the feeling of excitement. . . .

Mark was talking to Pat and Kathy. "I used to hang around in this café down by the seafront. This sister of mine, she used to sit and drink coffee there, day in, day out."

He was talking about Yarmouth.

"Where's your sister now?"

"She's in Brighton with Olson—that's the friend I'm going to meet. I haven't seen her in about a week."

"You coming with us to spend the night out on the beach?"

"Might as well, I s'pose. I got nowhere else to sleep."

Spud drove for a while without speaking. Eventually they came into the outskirts of Brighton. He grinned and began to slow down to a reasonable forty miles an hour. They drove in through the naked streets and past the shops. The lights of one or two shop windows were all that lit the roadway. The time was well past midnight. The streetlights were turned off now, and the streets were deserted.

Pat said, "Where are we stopping?"

"Along here." Spud turned onto the road which ran

parallel with the seafront and pointed ahead of him. The van sped on in the moonlight. Past the crowds of hippies sleeping beneath proverbial Brighton pier. Past a scattered couple of beach huts. Past an all-night café, and past a car park where people with frosted-up windows slept away the night and waited for morning.

The air was refreshing through the open windows. Chris sat up as Spud brought the van to a halt by the side of the road. Below them the sea lapped up against the beach, and to the right a gang of rockers or hippies lay talking and waiting for sleep around a transistor radio.

The doors opened and banged shut noisily as they clambered out of the van. Chris ran to the seawall and dropped down into the sand, a guitar and an unopened bottle of wine in his hands.

Spud was stretching after the long drive. Kathy was massaging her legs.

"Come on, let's get down on the beach."

"Sure, we're coming."

III

Chris stood, early the next morning, staring out hard at the white crests of the sea. He hadn't been to sleep all night. Lorraine stood by his side. They watched the waves and stood drinking still, as the sea began its slow, endless advance along the sands of the beach.

They'd been on the beach all night long. Pat and

34

Chris had stripped naked and gone for a swim. Lorraine stayed back on the sand for a while with Spud. Then she'd gone in for a swim, too. They left their clothes about a hundred yards away from the rockers/hippies over to their right, and then they moved away slightly to the left until they were almost out of sight.

Pat pulled at Chris' arm and dragged him out farther into the sea. They laughed at the sight of each other's bodies as they sank and swam in the cold water. Chris took Pat back into the shallows, and they lay facing the beach as the waves came up splashing over their backs and sometimes over their heads. He kissed her neck and her face through the salt water, and Lorraine laughed as Spud came into the water too and tried to comb his moustache.

The moonlight had been very faint so that it was almost dark, and through the darkness they could just make out the shapes of Mark and Kathy lying on the beach while the figures to the right lay trying to sleep.

Chris and Pat started to make love as the cold waves lapped over their bodies. Pat said, "We ought to use some sort of contraceptives."

Chris said, "Yeah," and Pat just laughed. She turned over onto her back, and he lay facing her in the same position as before. They could hear the noise of the transistor and, louder, the noise of Lorraine and Spud as they swore and splashed water at each other, behind them to the left.

35

Chris moved over onto Pat's body, slipped himself inside her below the water. Mark held one of the wine bottles to Kathy's lips, forced the hot wine down her throat. When it was over, Chris rolled over onto his back, lay there with the waves washing his body. He grabbed Pat by the arm and dragged her out again into the sea. They laughed and joked above the noise of the waves.

Eventually Mark and Kathy came into the water, too. Lorraine threw herself around Chris' neck. "Come on, then. Now make love to me."

She laughed. He said, "Let me have a rest for a minute then, and I'll fuck the whole world."

They splashed around in the water for another twenty minutes or so and then came out again onto the beach. The night air was cold, and they dried themselves quickly on coats and jumpers and started to get dressed.

Finally Spud got out the reefers, and they began to smoke. Inside the lightness of their heads, their brains floated with the clouds, and their minds clouded with the haze of delirium. The marijuana kept them alive, gave them new energy. They decided to save the rest of the wine for the morning.

Eventually they sat huddled in a circle on the beach, and someone handed Chris the guitar, and he played "Mr. Tambourine Man" for them, and they started to talk.

36

Lorraine sat on her leather jacket, and Kathy lay with her coat around her shoulders, smoking and trying to keep warm. Chris' eyes were far away on the horizon as he strummed on the guitar. No one spoke until he'd finished the song. There was a soft magic about it. The mystic formulation of the words. There seemed to be some kind of haunting message behind it, more because of the place they were hearing it than the way that it was being sung.

Pat looked into Chris' eyes as he finished. "That means a lot to you, that song, doesn't it?"

"Yeah, I s'pose it does."

"There's a lot of truth in some of these songs sometimes. You get a sudden feeling that you know exactly what they mean, exactly what they're saying. As if the song was written directly to you, and only you really understand it."

Chris nodded. "I know what you mean. I get like that with Dylan songs sometimes. But especially with this one. I can't explain it. It just gets me."

They shifted their positions slightly to keep warm. The night had gotten colder, and they talked on and on, their talk getting wilder and wilder with the effects of the marijuana.

"Someone once told me 'Mr. Tambourine Man' was the story of a junkie or a dope pusher. To him it was true because a song can mean anything to anyone. It just depends what you want it to mean. But as far as

I am concerned, he was talking a load of old crap. The way I see 'Mr. Tambourine Man,' it's like this: Dylan doesn't believe that paradise exists, and so he's creating a paradise of his own. Not for anyone else, but for himself. The boy who sings 'Mr. Tambourine Man' is trying to find that paradise, trying to gain admission to it.

" 'Mr. Tambourine Man' is the story of his attempt to get away from the world he sees around him. He sings it on some dark, dismal night when everyone else is asleep. There's some idea at the back of his mind, the idea of somewhere where all this won't matter. And yet at the same time he knows this idea is just something he himself has created, something which doesn't really exist. It's an expression of the attempt to find truth. But what happens when somebody does find it? They'd put him in an asylum and call him mad. And perhaps he would be." Chris closed his eyes, seemed to concentrate.

He said, "How could anyone hear 'Tambourine Man,' though, and not be moved by it? Like I said, Dylan doesn't believe in paradise, and he's creating a paradise of his own. It's the story of Dylan's search for peace as he lies in bed or wanders the streets of New York late one night, unable to sleep and probably feeling that if he can't manage to get away from everything soon, then he probably will go mad anyway."

Spud said, "Perhaps going mad is the only way you can find paradise."

38

Chris laughed. He said, "I reckon most people who do manage to create their own paradise probably get accused of going mad anyway—even if it's not true."

"Well, how can you define madness, anyway?"

"Yeah, you're right. It's impossible."

Lorraine said, "If you ask me, madness is the way we're feeling at the moment—high, on just a few wisps of bluish smoke. And in the same way that we realize we're high, then if you were insane you'd probably realize that too, and it wouldn't worry you—no more than being blocked worries us—because in your own way you'd probably be enjoying it."

Spud laughed, and Kathy lit herself a normal cigarette to make up for the fact that she had no share of the reefers.

Spud offered a reefer to her, but she shook her head. He offered it to Pat, and she took a slow puff on it and handed it back. About an hour later, Mark and Kathy moved off to sleep in the van, and Chris took Lorraine with him a bit farther up the beach.

They had lain there awake on the beach until morning, and then they had moved lazily down to the sea and stood there, watching the waves. Lorraine had brought a bottle of wine with her, and they started to drink. Lorraine wore her leather jacket, her name written on the back of it in great white diagonal letters.

"What's happened to Spud?"

"Dunno. He looks as if he's asleep."

"He must be getting old, can't take it anymore."

"Yeah." Lorraine grinned. She said, "Christ, I feel tired. We haven't had any sleep in over twenty-four hours."

They looked over to where Spud was lying, up against the seawall with Pat. He wasn't asleep, just lying there. He raised his hand, waved to them. Chris held up the wine, and Spud struggled up to stand with them by the sea.

"Give us a drink, then."

"Here."

He took a gulp of the wine and ran it around his dry mouth. "Christ, my mouth was dry."

"You should've come and got something before. There's another two bottles."

Spud nodded. "Yeah, I could have, I s'pose. Where's Mark and Kathy got to?"

"They're still in the van."

Spud said, "You know this Olson that Mark's come down to see? Has Mark told you anything about him?"

"No, why?"

"Well, he was telling me about him last night. This Olson is some kind of religious maniac. He has this little sect of believers around him who all think he's the Saviour."

"Chris said, "Oh, Christ, no."

"Yeah, it's true. He's got some name for himself. I can't remember what it was now, but it means the De-

40

liverer or something like that. Man, it's crazy. They reckon this Olson's a hypnotist and a mind reader. Really insane."

"What the hell's Mark going down to see him for, then?"

"Mark's one of the believers, I s'pose. I don't really know. When he was telling me about it, he sounded as if he really believed every word. First of all, I thought he was joking, but he was dead serious. Like I said, it's crazy."

Chris took another swig of the wine and stretched his arms. They turned around and walked back to the seawall. Pat was lying there in a shallow sleep. They woke her up, and Chris put on his reefer jacket and picked up his guitar.

"What's the time?"

"It's about seven o'clock."

"We gonna walk down to the town, get ourselves something to eat?"

"Yeah. Let's go and wake up the others."

They woke the others and started walking off into the center of Brighton. Chris and Lorraine thought about Olson and grinned to each other and to Spud as they walked along. But they didn't say anything, and the conversation lapsed.

They found a café at about half past seven and waited for it to open. Inside, a man turned on lights and unbolted the door. They went in and got something to eat. When they left, it was almost half past eight. They walked toward the pier and sat down for a little while on the beach. The whole of Brighton seemed to be deserted. No one spoke, and no one moved. At nine they heard a clock strike somewhere on a far distant church tower, and after about another forty minutes they walked toward the amusement arcades and mingled with the gathering crowds.

Chris bought a hat, played the slot machines, and ate grapes. They wandered around for about two hours. A group of people pointed Chris out as they walked along the streets, and it reminded him of the episode in Oscar Wilde's *Dorian Gray* where two young gentlemen noticed Dorian Gray walking home one night and began to whisper scandal about him below their breath. Chris wondered if he'd ever get to feel like Dorian Gray— hating to be recognized, dressing up in old clothes so that he could go to the East End opium dens unnoticed. He put another grape into his mouth and thought about something else. Obscurity would come quickly enough by itself without chasing it. He didn't need fame and recognition, but he didn't need obscurity either. So why worry about it? If he worried he got depressed, and depression came quickly enough by itself, too. Too quickly, in fact.

They walked through one of the shops, looking at postcards. Mark said, "I s'pose I ought to start looking for Olson."

"I thought you said he'd find you."

"Yeah, I s'pose he will. Why don't we go to the pier?"

"Yeah, all right. We might as well."

They sat on a seat on the pier. Mark looked over to his right suddenly. "Hey, it's Olson."

He gestured to Olson. "I had a feeling he might be here."

Olson walked over to him. He was the strangest-looking man in the world. Spud guessed that the girl by his side must be Mary, Mark's sister. Mark stood up and announced everybody's names. Olson insisted on shaking hands. As he shook hands with Chris, he looked directly into his eyes. Chris was certain that Olson's eyes were the deepest red. Shaking hands with Olson seemed to last an age. He was conscious of nothing but the eyes, the red eyes. When it was over, Chris lit a cigarette. Olson stood talking with Mark and his sister. It sounded like just friendly chitchat, a discussion of the journey down, a family reunion.

Chris offered Olson a cigarette. He refused. Mark and Mary took one, and he gave them his box of matches. Mary looked more or less the same as she had when Chris had seen her before. He studied her, wondered what she was doing here with Olson. Then he looked back at Olson himself. He couldn't stop himself looking at the eyes again. How the hell could anyone have eyes that color? The color was indescribable, as if the eyes were burning, as if any moment his whole forehead was likely to go up in flames.

Chris looked around at Lorraine. He made an excuse, and they went off to buy a couple of ice creams. They flopped down into deck chairs as soon as they were out of sight.

Chris said, "What d'you think of him?"

"Olson?"

"Yeah."

"Nothing much. I reckon he must be a nut."

He laughed, and they got their ice creams and walked back. Spud was sitting down still. Mary was sitting next to him, and Mark and Olson were still standing up. Pat and Kathy had started talking to each other. They looked bored.

Mark said, "It's about time we went. Thanks for the lift and everything."

Spud shrugged. "It's all right, man. We'll see you again sometime."

"Yeah, I'll see you around. We got a flat in Wandsworth. Allfarthing Lane, number one. Come and see us sometime."

"Sure."

Olson nodded to them. He watched Chris studiously for a minute, and then he walked away.

2. / *And Aftermath*

THEY walked around until about seven and then returned to the van. The sky had come over cloudy, and it looked as if it were going to rain. They sat in the back of the van for a while, talking, and then they decided to drive out into the country somewhere and find a pub.

Chris was quiet while they were driving. Lorraine went to sleep and the other three talked, but Chris stayed quiet. He was beginning to feel tired. It was almost forty hours now since he'd been to sleep. He looked down at Lorraine and wished he could fall asleep. Everything seemed to irritate him—the noise of the van, the chatter and talk from the others, the drifting smoke from their cigarettes. He settled down against the door and made himself comfortable. He'd felt exactly the same feelings inside him about four weeks ago. He'd lain in bed somewhere, in some small hotel room in Croydon, trying to get to sleep, thinking, wondering. That had been the start of it all, the start of the periods of depression he'd been feeling.

Chris tried to analyze his own feelings. He knew that he was starting to feel irritated, starting to get depressed, and yet he couldn't do anything to stop himself. It was as if he were a completely different person, noticing his own feelings but having no control over them. It was almost as if—fuck it. What did it matter? Who the hell cared, anyway? He lit himself another cigarette.

They turned off the main road and drove on.

Kathy said, "You got any idea where we're going?"

Spud shook his head. He said, "I'm just driving till we get out in the country. We'll get to some little village or something. Then we can find a pub."

"We ain't gonna have much room for sleeping tonight, not if we're sleeping in the van."

"It won't be all that bad. Someone can sleep up here in the front. The rest of us can sleep in the back."

Chris said, "Aw, I don't wanna sleep out for another night. Why don't we drive back to London?"

"You don't wanna go back yet, do ya? We can sleep out tonight and then drive back tomorrow."

Pat was laughing. "Yeah, let's have another night. We don't wanna get stranded up in London."

Chris shrugged. He said, "Well, wait till we get to

46

the pub. We can work out what we wanna do then."
He stretched out, almost full length, on the floor of the
van. Pat laid herself out with her head in his lap, massaging his leg. They drove on, fields and scattered
houses on either side of the road. Spud started talking
again.

"Hey, you ever read any of the Marquis de Sade?"

"I read a few odd bits, nothing much."

"Christ, that bloke had a filthy mind!" Spud laughed.
"I read a few of his books about a year ago. It takes you
about half an hour to understand what he's getting at,
but Christ, he must have been sex mad."

The conversation was interrupted and half lost in
the noises of the van. Chris and Pat kept quiet, and
Lorraine slept on uneasily. Chris could hear an odd
word here and there, through the interruption:

"I reckon if you wanna spend your life testing out
other people's perversions, then it's up to you. The
only real thing De Sade ever did wrong was giving his
honest opinions on the French Revolution and saying
a few nasty things about Napoleon Bonaparte. If it
wasn't for his fucking political writing, then hardly
anyone would have worried about him. As far as De
Sade's sex life was concerned, they just used it as an excuse to put him in some bloody prison somewhere to
keep him out of the way."

"Perhaps it's a good job they did. If he hadn't been

in prison, he probably would've been out raping people instead of staying inside and writing about it. And then you wouldn't have had any sex books to read."

"You're right, man, I wouldn't. I'd have had to go out and rape people myself."

The van rocked from side to side on the narrow country road. "I think there's probably a village up here," Spud said. They passed a group of houses and a pub. Spud drove on to the end of the village and stopped by the side of the road. Chris woke up Lorraine.

"Come on, we're there."

She woke up, opened her eyes. "Where are we?"

Spud said, "Out in the country somewhere. We just passed a pub."

Lorraine said, "We need some fags. We'd better get some at this pub." She looked at Chris. He nodded slowly.

Spud said, "We were gonna sleep the night in the van and start back home tomorrow."

"Aw, let's drive on home tonight," Chris said. "I don't wanna sleep the night in this bloody van."

Lorraine laughed. "It'll be all right. It's not as cramped as all that." She put her hand on Chris' shoulder. He turned around and looked out of the back window of the van. His head was aching, splitting.

Pat started talking. Pat and Lorraine laughed again. Spud made some comment about De Sade, and there was more laughter.

Lorraine moved over to Chris.

"What's the matter?"

He said, "Come on, let's get out of here and get those bloody fags."

They got out onto the road. Chris left his coat in the back of the van. He started to walk off up the road. Lorraine turned to Spud. "You coming?"

"Yeah, we'll come along in a minute. We'll see ya in the pub."

Lorraine nodded and started to follow Chris. She was wearing her leather jacket still, and slung over her shoulders she had Kathy's raincoat. Chris was about five yards in front. She caught up with him. He was quiet. He walked along, just looking directly in front of him, not speaking.

It was cold. Lorraine pulled the raincoat tighter around her shoulders. She looked at Chris. "You cold?"

He shook his head.

They walked through the village. The houses were large and old. They passed a red telephone box on the other side of the road. The wind seemed to blow right through them along the narrow street. They walked on to the pub. Chris turned to her. "You'd better get the fags. I don't wanna go in there."

He waited outside while she went to get the cigarettes. He put his hand up to his head. A sort of pain. Dullness. Sickness. Lorraine came back outside.

He said, "Look, you might as well go back in the

pub and wait for the others. I just wanna go for a walk, up along this road."

"I'll come with you."

"You don't have to."

"I'll come."

He turned and started to walk. She walked behind him for a while. They didn't say anything. Eventually she came and walked beside him. There was no pavement, so they walked on the edge of the road. She gave him a cigarette, and they lit it in the wind. Chris said, "I'm not coming back to sleep in that van tonight. I'll sleep out around here somewhere, then early tomorrow morning I'm gonna start hitchhiking back to London."

"Why?"

"I wanna be by myself for a while. I don't know why, I just do."

They passed an old church, fields and woods on either side of the road. Chris stopped by the side of the road and sat down on the grass. A car passed them, and then a lorry. Chris buried his head in his hands. The first cigarette was finished, and he lit himself a second one. He closed his eyes, his hand on his forehead again.

"You're tired."

"It's not that." The words seemed to snap out angrily.

She talked softly. She said, "What is it, then?"

"I don't know. Why do you always have to disagree with everything I want to do? I want to drive home tonight, so you say you want to stay here. I wanna do one thing, and you always wanna do something else. Why d'you always have to disagree with me in front of other people, make me feel like I'm your bloody husband or something, who always has to do everything because you do it?" He threw the cigarette away into the road. Tears began to collect in the corners of his eyes. He sat up, looked out at the wet landscape. The wind hit him in the face, blew at his hair. He breathed heavily, looked up toward the sky.

They lay there for twenty minutes. Chris turned over, face downward, his head in the long grass. His mind was confused, unable to think. He felt sorry, angry, muddled, confused. Lorraine moved nearer to him, put her arms around his neck, drew him up toward her. He moved away again. He didn't want to kiss her. He didn't want to do anything.

He said, "That doesn't do any good."

"Why?"

"You kiss, and then you stop kissing. And it doesn't solve anything."

She dropped down again into the grass. He said, "You might as well go back to the pub with the others. I'll be all right."

He stood up and started to walk on. Lorraine followed him. He looked around at her face, but her eyes were focused ahead of her. Lorraine began to shiver. They walked for about five minutes. It had started to rain. He could feel the tears welling up in his eyes. Oh, Christ, he didn't want to hurt her. He didn't see why she should have to go through it all, too. But why didn't she realize, why didn't she understand, why didn't she treat him like—oh, what did it matter?

There was a pain directly over his eyes. He ignored it. The rain was starting to get heavy, but he didn't seem to notice.

Lorraine pulled the coat around her. She was shivering. They had left the village behind them, out of sight.

"You must be freezing."

He just shook his head. They walked on for another couple of minutes. Lorraine lit two more cigarettes, shivering still. He said, "We'd better walk back. You're gonna freeze."

They turned and walked back. The wind blew at them from behind, and the rain drove down on them. But they walked slowly. They didn't speak. They walked in silence, Chris with his eyes closed, concentrating, the cigarette in his mouth.

Lorraine said, "Why don't ya wanna sleep in the van?"

"I just wanna go mad quietly, by myself, that's all. Without Spud and all the others being there to help me."

"And what about me?"

He turned to her, lowered his eyes, and just shook his head, refusing to speak.

She took one side of the coat and put it around his shoulder. The wind blew at his hair still and blew the rain onto his shirt.

"I'm not cold."

Lorraine held the coat where it was, over his shoulder. "It's raining. You'll get soaked."

He said, "Yeah, but it's inside me that I'm worried about, not outside."

She pulled him nearer to her, and he put his arm weakly around her waist. He could feel his face wet with the rain and warm with his tears. They walked in silence for about eight minutes until they saw the church again. Chris said, "Oh, Christ, I don't know what's the matter with me." He looked at Lorraine. "But it ain't you. Not really. It's just that I feel—oh, I don't know. Everything's too much, everything's horrible. There's no fucking point in anything. I'd feel better if I was dead."

She gripped him a little more tightly, and they continued walking. The rain came down in torrents. They passed the pub again and walked on. Ahead of them there was a telephone box.

"Give me another fag."

She handed him the cigarette packet. He lit a cigarette and gave her back the packet. He walked over toward the telephone box, and they went inside it, out of the rain. They stood there, the water dripping off them onto the floor. Chris buried his head again in his hands. A feeling of helplessness, nothingness. What could he do? Why couldn't he just die, fade away into the rain? He looked up at his face in the telephone-box mirror. His hair was everywhere, and streaks of water ran from the corners of his eyes to the corners of his mouth. He saw the reflection of Lorraine standing behind him. He leaned himself against her body, his head bowed against her neck. She put her arms around him, held him tight. He could feel that she was crying, too. He didn't know what about, he didn't even know what he was crying about himself.

They stood there like that for a few minutes. The cigarette burned down and dropped from Chris' fingers. Lorraine took out the cigarette packet and lit two more. She looked into his eyes as she lit the cigarettes. She wanted to talk, but she didn't know what to say. She took a long drag on her cigarette, handed the other one to Chris. He took it and turned away. His whole throat seemed to be blocked up; his headache had gotten worse. He opened the door of the telephone box and spat out into the rain. The wind was refreshing. He stood there with the door open for a moment, just breathing. Then he shut the door again, turned back toward Lorraine.

"You all right?"

"I don't know. I don't even know what's the matter. He took hold of her hand. "Oh, Christ, I think I must be going mad. I'm getting so upset over this bloody little argument. So many stupid trivialities. Everything builds up in my mind as if I just couldn't stand it all anymore. I feel as if everything is going rotten. I can't think anymore. I'm just a living smoke machine, filling myself with nicotine and slowly rotting away. I've got this bloody headache right between my eyes and a bloody pain in my stomach making me feel I want to be sick. Oh, Christ." He put his hand to his head again. "You might as well go over to the pub. Leave me here. I'll be all right."

"I don't wanna go over there. I'll stay here with you."

He looked up into her face. "You sure?"

"Yeah, I'm sure."

He collapsed against her, his arms around her waist. "I don't really want you to go away, Lorraine. I'm sorry about before."

"I know. We'll sleep out somewhere tonight. Just the two of us. Tomorrow we can get back to London."

He looked out at the rain. He nodded. She said, "We'd better go back to the van, get your coat."

"Yeah." They walked out into the rain. Chris could hardly walk. He almost fell over. Lorraine laughed weakly. She took hold of his hand, and they walked through the rain. He looked over at her. He said, "You don't have to sleep out with me tonight if you don't want to. I just wanna get away for a bit, get away from all the talk and the shouting. But it's probably gonna be cold and wet all night. I don't care because I'm not really thinking about it, but you'll freeze. If you wanna stay here in the van, then you might as well. I wouldn't be much company for ya, anyway."

"I don't care about that. I'd rather be with you."

They reached the van and sat in the back, the doors flung open to the wind. A puddle of rainwater lay below them in the road. Rain splashed against the windows of the van. Lorraine said, "We better find ourselves somewhere out of the rain."

"There was a tractor shed back along the road, in the farmyard."

"Yeah, I saw it. It looked a bit muddy, but it'd be dry probably."

They lay back in the van for a while. Chris said, "You took your pill today?"

"Yeah." She laughed. "I took it before we left Brighton."

They sat, saying nothing, watching the rain. The time was about a quarter past ten. Chris got his coat, slung it around his shoulders. Lorraine kept Kathy's coat and her own leather jacket. They walked back along the road. Chris closed his eyes with the pain of the headache. He wanted to cry—there was nothing to be ashamed of—but there were no tears left.

They joined hands and reached the pub. Just as they got there, they heard the sound of Pat and Kathy coming out of the door.

"Hi. We been waiting for you. We wondered where you'd got to."

"Oh, we just been walking." Lorraine looked around for Spud. "Where's Spud?"

"He's behind us. He's just coming."

"Oh. We'll see ya later on."

Pat and Kathy walked back toward the van. They waited for Spud. Spud said, "Hi, Chris, Lorraine. You all right?"

"Yeah, we're all right. We're not gonna come back to the van tonight, Spud. We're gonna walk for a bit and sleep out for the night."

"What the hell for? You'll soak."

"I just wanna get away for a bit, Spud. We'll see you all in the morning."

"Okay, man. If that's what you want," Spud shrugged.

II

They walked off a little way. Lorraine said, "Let's get something to drink out of that pub."

"You get something if you want. I don't want anything."

"Get a couple of bottles of orange or something. We can drink them during the night."

He went into the pub and got two bottles of still orange. He took a sip from the top of one of the orange bottles, and they walked on along the road, holding their orange under their coats, out of the rain. It was dark, and the rain was heavy still. They reached the entrance to the farmyard by the side of the road.

"We're there. Let's go and have a look, see if there's anywhere we can sleep."

"We need a torch or something. How many matches you got?"

"I've got half a box. You'd better be careful, striking matches around here, though. There might be petrol around out of those tractors."

"Yeah."

The shed was large, open-ended and made of wood. They moved between the two tractors and struck a match. Chris took off his wet coat and left it on the wheel of one of the tractors.

"Christ, I can't see a thing."

"There's room just here. What's over there?"

"Nothing. A load of tires and old cans. We might as well stay where we are."

"Hold the orange. I'll shake out this coat, and we can use it as a groundsheet."

"Wait a minute. I've found some canvas or something." He dragged the green canvas over to Lorraine, and she spread it out on the ground between the two tractors. There wasn't much room, but they shook out their coats, stretched out on the canvas, and pulled the coats up over the top of them. Chris kicked off his shoes. The time was getting close to eleven o'clock. A car went past on the road outside, but they were hidden by the two tractors, and the car's headlights passed over their heads.

Lorraine said, "You feeling any better now?"

"Yeah, I feel a bit better. I got that headache still, though. I got a funny taste in my mouth, too. I could do with a drink of orange." He sat up to get the two orange bottles, and between them they finished up the two drinks. He rolled the two bottles away again, behind one of the tractors. Lorraine turned over to face him. She ran her hand along the inside of his leg. His hand moved over to her thighs, inside her shirt and along her spine.

"Oh, Christ, you're sending shivers right up my back."

"You're sending shivers right up my front."

"They laughed. "Perhaps I'd better stop doing it, then."

"Fucking hell. You'd better not."

He opened her shirt, kissed her on the top of her breast.

"Take my bra off for me. Christ, I can feel meself getting wet."

He grinned and said, "It must be raining again."

"I don't think it's rain. It's between my legs."

Chris lay down on the ground, and she sat up so that he could undo her bra. "Christ, that thing was killing me." She laughed to herself. She said, "What if a bloody copper was to come along now? It'd be like that time on Clacton beach all over again."

Thinking about it made Chris smile. He said, "You remember the trial? That fucking judge? And the time we was in that beach hut, hiding from the police?"

"Yeah, I remember it. We found a couple of blankets, and we had to move the table out of the way so we'd have room to lie down on the floor."

Chris felt Lorraine's hand on his legs again. He pulled her down onto the ground again, and they kissed. Her body was warm. She pulled out his shirt from the top of his jeans and started to undo the buttons.

"You know something? I haven't wanted it as bad as this for about four weeks."

"Christ, get yourself undressed quickly. I can't wait much longer."

"I've got a bloody headache, remember. I gotta take things easy."

She tossed back her hair. "I've got a pain over me eyes, too. Seems to be just over on one side. I must've caught it from you." She laughed again. "As long as that's all I catch, though, I don't mind."

He grinned weakly, almost unhappily. He didn't want to talk anymore—not if it was just making conversation, just chattering. He ran his hand over his forehead again. They took off their jeans, got undressed, keeping their shirts on because of the cold.

Chris felt the warmth of her body beneath him. He did everything instinctively, automatically. But there was nothing in it. It was like eating a meal not because you were hungry but just because it was available, just because it happened to be there. He pulled himself away again as soon as it was over. Lorraine's whole body heaved, and then she flopped down, breathing heavily, onto the ground. She said, "Oh, my Christ. It was like a load of explosions or something going off inside me. Like someone squeezing a bloody tomato right up inside my body." She stretched her arms, lying there, recovering her breath. Chris reached out for the cigarette packet, lit a couple of cigarettes. They smoked in silence for a while.

Then Chris said, "Did you ever have sex anytime and suddenly just get the feeling halfway through that it was all just sickening and not even worth doing?"

"How d'you mean?"

"I don't know. A feeling that really you don't even want it. Right in the middle of it all, not before or after, but right in the middle."

"Is that how you felt then?"

He nodded. He said, "It's nothing to do with you. It was just me."

She said, "It's funny. For me it was fucking marvelous. For you it was bloody nothing."

"It was sort of strange. Before we got undressed, you were getting me worked up, and everything was all right. Then suddenly I felt strange again. I had my headache and I felt sick, and half of me wanted to make love to you and have an orgasm and all the rest of it, while the other half of me just wanted to be sick. It was like when you lie in bed at night, and you can't get to sleep, so you just lie there, masturbating, and in the end you get to the point where you don't really want it anymore, anyway. It makes you feel like a bloody twelve-year-old kid. And that was how I felt just now. It was like my body didn't even want it anymore, just my brain. And when it was over, my brain was just sickened with itself, and the body was lying there with the coats sticking to it, exhausted."

"I never felt it, but I know what you mean."

He turned over to put his arm around her. He said, "I never felt like that before. It was sort of horrible, frightening, like everything had gone rotten on me, even sex."

"It doesn't mean anything, though. It's just 'cos you're tired. You do everything in extremes. Like not sleeping for about forty-eight hours and getting yourself so depressed that you end up having to get away from everybody and needing to be alone. You'll be all right in the morning. You just need to get to sleep."

"I think I need to stop myself thinking so much,

stop myself worrying." He wanted to talk on, but he couldn't find the words.

She glanced up, looked outside. It was raining again. They were in the farmyard. Opposite them was what looked like a barn. The night was dark, and she could hardly see. On their left there was a road, and on their right there was grass or trees. She turned back to Chris. "You wanna talk, or d'ya wanna try to go to sleep?"

"Let's talk. We should've saved some of that orange. These fags are gonna make our mouths dry. I feel I want something else to drink already."

"We could always drink rainwater."

He grimaced for a moment in the darkness. "I don't feel that thirsty."

She said, "You know, I reckon you must be hooked on water. You drink more in a day than most other people drink in a month."

"I know. I can't help it. I have to drink something or I'd just dry up."

Another car went past them, its headlights flashing over the dirt and paint of the two tractors.

"Move that coat over this way a bit."

"Give me a bit more room, then."

They shifted their positions and hid themselves under the two coats.

"Christ, it's bloody cold."

"Yeah, I know."

Lorraine said, "Why don't we go off for a few weeks' holiday? Somewhere quiet."

"I got a book of bloody engagements to fill before I can do anything like that. Spud reckons I've gotta be in Manchester in a couple of days."

"And what you got after that?"

"Oh, I don't know. Just the same thing, but in different towns. I do a tour of Scotland or something in a few weeks' time."

"You could cancel some of the engagements."

"Yeah, I could do, I s'pose. But it's not that that makes me so tired. If I didn't sing, then I'd feel more depressed than ever. I don't feel tired when I'm singing, and anyway, this tour of Scotland should be good. There's some American disc jockey coming with us, and the Representative, and a load of others. I've been wanting to go back to Edinburgh for months, ever since I was up there last summer."

"How long's this tour gonna last, then?" Lorraine said.

"I think it's about four weeks. I'm not sure, though. Spud's got the dates written down somewhere. We start at the end of this month and finish up in Glasgow at the end of September. We have four or five free days in Edinburgh in the middle of the tour, I think. Apart from that it's all working and traveling around."

"Do you want me to come with you?"

"You've gotta be in Stevenage to see your parents."

Lorraine swore. "Oh, Christ. Yeah, I'd forgotten."

They heard noises as someone walked past, along the road. There was the sound of two pairs of shoes grating on the pavement. Chris sat up and tried to look at Lorraine. It was so dark that he could hardly see her. The shoes walked on without stopping, and he lay down again. His face was covered by wet, dark brown hair. He said, "I thought it might be a copper or something."

Lorraine brushed the hair away from his eyes. "I can only just see ya," she said.

"It's this tractor. It keeps the light off us." He pulled the coat up over him again. "Aren't ya getting cold like that?"

"I'm all right, I got you to keep me warm."

He said, "I won't keep ya very warm. I'm freezing myself."

She pushed her cold hand between his legs. "You feel warm to me." Her hand rested in his crutch. "Give me a kiss."

He turned over onto his side and kissed her. She held him tight. He could feel the excitement running through his body. The sensations of sex running from his brain to his toes. He could hear the conflicting voices speaking softly inside him. He felt apart from it all, completely detached. Lorraine's mouth broke away gently from his, slithered across his face and then onto his neck, breathing harshly. He could feel her body there beside him, nothing but her body. The bare flesh of her legs moved against the light-colored hairs of his own. He could feel her hands, her arms.

He moved his own arms into position, underneath and above her body. He ran his right hand slowly along the length of her back, down to the base of her spine, over the two humps of her backside and then along the slim insides of her legs. Lorraine moaned softly. He glanced down at her breasts. She moved nearer, and he kissed them. Her hands were everywhere. He pressed himself against them, moved himself against her body. He felt her fingers as they slid over his thighs, found his stomach, slid quickly through the tense pubic hair.

She drew him on top of her, and he found the two thick lips between her legs, massaged them with his fingers. He heard her whispering, "Oh, Christ. Oh, Christ." He pushed open her legs. He knew there was only one thought in the whole of his existence. He fucked her quickly. Nothing else mattered to him, nothing else counted, there was nothing else in the whole world . . . and then suddenly it was over. The thing came almost as a shock to him. Lorraine moved on still beneath him. She hadn't finished, she breathed heavily still, moaned.

Chris lay there on top of her. He hardly moved. His face was beside hers, facing the ground. His mouth was by her ear. Hair—his or hers—got in his eyes and brushed against his tongue. He felt an overwhelming tiredness, desperation. He closed his eyes.

Lorraine was motionless suddenly. There was silence for a second, and then she lifted up his head and looked into his face. She made as if she were going to kiss him. The tongue came inside his mouth, hair jammed between their lips. Chris moved away. He could feel the horrible stickiness, the trail of wetness which would be running from between her legs. He sat up, tried to arrange the coats again. He said, "It's no good, Lorraine. God, let me try to get to sleep, let me get to sleep."

They lay with their arms around each other, half dressed and with the coats pulled over them, for almost forty minutes. The time was late, and the rain was forming a puddle outside the shed. Eventually they fell asleep. Chris dreamed for a while and slept until about three o'clock in the morning. He woke with a start. He turned around to Lorraine and saw that she was awake, too. She was lying there, smoking. Chris lit himself a cigarette and buried himself against Lorraine. They talked for a while and smoked two more cigarettes.

It was the coldest time of the whole night, and as soon as they'd finished smoking, they started trying to get back to sleep. Chris slept till half past four, fell asleep again and woke up at half past five.

It was light by now. He could read the time on the

clock on the tower of the church. He lay there for a few moments, wishing he could get back to sleep. In the end he sat up and lit himself a cigarette and then disappeared again beneath the coat. It was cold still. The rain had stopped, but it was cold. Chris smoked and lay there until ten minutes to six. Lorraine was asleep still. He pulled his clothes across to him and got himself quickly dressed.

He stood up and did up the buttons of his shirt. He covered Lorraine with her own clothes and Kathy's coat and put his coat on himself. The coat was dusty, muddy. He pushed his hands deep into the pockets and walked out to look around him. The rain had left puddles in the mud, but the sun was shining very weakly over the small farmyard. Chris stood for a moment, taking in the scene all around him. He turned around and walked down to the road. He stood there for almost five minutes. The farmhouse was on the side of the road opposite to them, partly hidden by another barn. The streets were silent and empty. He walked back to the shed with the two tractors. Lorraine was asleep still. She would be cold when she woke up. He might as well let her sleep on.

He sat down on the wheel of one of the tractors. The scene made him feel happy. He lit another cigarette and imagined what he must look like, sitting there. In front of him there was a small pond, and around the sides of the pond there were a few trees.

The sun was streaming through the trees and through the grass. It was very weak, but the sight of it was refreshing to him at that moment. He smiled. It was the first time he'd really smiled in about twelve hours. He sat there for almost twenty minutes. His coat and his jeans had gotten filthy. He inspected them uninterestedly. He turned up the collar of his coat and waited for Lorraine to wake up.

She stirred herself finally and turned over on the hard canvas. He walked toward her and stood over her, leaning against one of the tractors. She turned around again and glanced up at him through her sleepy eyes. He said, "It's about quarter past six. Don't rush. Get up when you're ready."

She yawned. She said, "How long you been up?"

"Not long. 'Bout half an hour."

He walked away again and sat down on the wheel of the tractor. Lorraine put on her jeans and her leather jacket and slung the coat back over her shoulder. They started to walk off, and she said, "How you feeling?"

He shrugged. He said, "It's not so bad now. I think I've got over most of it. My throat's dry still, that's all."

They reached the road and started to walk back in the direction of the van.

3. / *Wait Outside the Hall*

THREE weeks later he sat in Edinburgh. It was the start of the tour, and the first performance was just over. He sat in the dressing room; Pete Steward of the Representative sat with him. They had escaped from the American, Bob Deene, about ten minutes before. Deene pushed open the door and strode into the dressing room. "How d'you think it went?"

Pete said, "Great, great."

Chris said, "Yeah, great," and looked down again at the open note pad on his knee.

Deene said, "We're all going back to the hotel. There's a bit of a party going on. You two coming?"

Pete shook his head. "We got an idea for a song. We're trying to get it written down. We thought we'd go and get a cup of coffee somewhere, come back to the hotel later on."

Deene backed toward the door. "Sure, I'll see ya in the morning." He opened the door and then bobbed back again. "Oh, by the way, the big boss has changed the schedule. We only have one more night in Edinburgh. Then we drive straight to Dunfermline and spend tomorrow night there."

They nodded absently. "Yeah, okay. Thanks for telling us."

Deene disappeared, and Chris flapped shut the notebook and said, "You fancy going and getting some coffee?"

"Yeah, come on." They picked up their coats and walked to the door. The ballroom was almost empty. They walked out past the stage and over toward the street door. Pete said, "I know a place around the corner, stays open all night."

They chatted as they walked along.

"Did ya see that girl pressed up against the front of the stage? She was there while you were onstage, wearing a pink skirt, short hair."

"Yeah, I saw her. I reckon she was after Dave. I saw 'em talking together about ten o'clock."

They passed a clothes shop, glanced in at the windows. People walked past them along the streets—students, hippies and intellectuals up for the Edinburgh Festival, boys looking for girls, girls looking for boys. They walked on to the café and bought themselves coffee. Pete got himself something to eat. "How d'you feel about this song?"

"I dunno. Let's read through what we've got. Yeah, I reckon it's quite good, only we can't do much more till we work out the rest of the tune. We can do it to-morrow morning. We can work it out on guitars and then get Dave or someone to write it all down for us."

"Yeah, I don't fancy writing it down meself. I get meself tied up in knots, trying to write music."

They both grinned.

"Jeff said you'd gotta do a TV show on Saturday."

"Yeah, we've gotta make a recording for some show next week. We haven't been on television now for about six weeks. Ray thought it was about time we had a few more plugs."

Chris said, "I wouldn't have thought you needed 'em. You went down almost as well tonight as you did that time in the Marquee Club about eighteen months ago. You remember that? Christ, it was a riot."

"Yeah," Pete said. "It makes us sound bloody old, don't it? We've been going now for over twenty months. If you ask me, people are gonna put up with the groups for about another six months, and then they're gonna just tell 'em that"—he raised two fingers —"tell us to go to hell."

"I dunno. You've got something to say, and you say it. I don't see what difference it makes if there's five of you standing up on the stage or just one of you. Sure, a lot of the groups are gonna die, but not all of them. All the old Merseyside groups are dead anyway, but there's still lots of other groups surviving."

Pete said, "Aw, it's not that I'm being cynical. It's just that I think most of these groups are content to churn out the same old rubbish time after time, record after record, without even bothering to change the strings on their guitars. Now people like you, you can do more or less what you want. You can write your own songs, and you can sing what you want to sing. But we're caught up in a trend. So when the trend dies out, we'll probably die with it. Look at the billing for this tour. We're starting to die already. You're top of the bill, not us."

"Yeah, but think back to the first time we ever met each other, almost two years ago. You were one of the most popular groups out, and I was just something that had crawled out of a courtroom."

Pete laughed. He said, "By the way, I saw Napoleon the other day. It was about a week ago, down in London. He said he wanted to see ya."

"What'd he wanna see me about?"

"Oh, I dunno. Nothing important. It was just that he hadn't seen you for a few months, I think."

Chris lit a cigarette. After they'd had another coffee, they left and went walking again, through the neon

74

streets. They walked with their coats slung loosely over their shoulders and their hands in their pockets, talking. On a street corner they met a couple of girls. There was some talk and the exchange of one of the girls' cigarettes. They talked for some time, and then the girls took them to a bowling alley, and they sat in the Wimpy Bar.

Chris said to the girls, "Hey, you never told us your names."

"My name's Edwina, but they call me Jacky."

Pete said, "How old are ya?"

"Eighteen."

"You ain't."

"No, really we're fifteen."

"What the hell'd you say you were eighteen for?"

"I dunno. Thought you wouldn't be interested, I s'pose, if ya knew we was fifteen." She blew smoke up into the air and laughed.

"Christ, what the hell does age matter? People are just people. It doesn't matter what age they are."

"No, I know. But some boys won't go out with ya if ya tell 'em you're only fifteen."

"I knew a girl, Susan her name was, she got talking to some American down by Trafalgar Square. He was twenty-five years old, and he was married. Every five seconds he kept looking over at me and saying, 'Don't tell her how old I am. Don't tell her I'm married.'

Christ, how bloody stupid! He seemed to think if she knew how old he was, she wouldn't have been interested."

Pete said, "Who was that? The Susan who came from Lancashire?"

Chris said, "Yeah. She was nineteen. That sort of thing was happening to her all the time. The first week she arrived in Stevenage, she went to the pictures with some boy who was seventeen. He spent the whole evening worrying about whether he should tell her he was younger than she was or not."

One of the girls started combing her hair. Jacky was dark-haired, with a short mod haircut. Carol's hair was the same, but fair. They wore two identical skirts, one blue and one red.

Chris sat with his chair wedged against the wall. He dawdled absently on the table with his fingers. Pete sat with Jacky and chain-smoked four cigarettes. The bowling alley stayed open till three o'clock in the morning, and people wandered past them on their way between the bowling lanes and the Wimpy Bar, their laughter mingling with the sounds of the jukebox.

Pete got up and put on a Rolling Stones record. They sat listening to it in silence. Carol said suddenly, "Christ, I've got a sweaty crutch." All four of them burst into laughter.

Chris said, "There must be a bloody joke in that somewhere, but I'm not gonna tell it."

"I heard a joke the other day," Pete said. "This bloke was walking around the streets of Paris, ya see, and he went into some brothel. The trouble was that he hadn't got much money. So he went up to the woman in charge of this brothel, and he said, 'I've come along for a bit of sex, but the trouble is that I've only got five shillings on me.'

"So this woman said, 'Well, I can't let you go with one of the girls if all you've got is five bob, but if you go into that room over there, I'll let you have it away with my pet kangaroo.'

"The bloke thinks to himself, 'Well, I might as well try it. It's only gonna cost me five bob.' So he goes into the room, takes off his clothes, and has it away with this kangaroo.

"The next week he comes back to this brothel, and this time he's only got two and six. So he goes up to the woman, and he says the same thing again: 'I've come along for a bit of sex, but all I can afford is two and six.' So the woman says to him, 'Right, give me your two and six, and you can go into that room at the end of the corridor and look through the hole in the wall.'

"So he gives her his money, and he goes along to this room at the end of the corridor. He opens the door, and he sees all these blokes standing, looking through these holes in the wall. So he goes and looks through one of these holes, and he sees this woman lying on the bed in the next room, with nothing on except her bra. Then some bloke comes along and gets on the bed with her, and she starts taking his clothes off for him. She gets all his clothes off for him, and they mess around for a while. Then the bloke lays her down on the bed and has it away with her.

"When they've finished, the bloke who's watching it through the hole in the wall is almost sweating. He turns around to the bloke next to him, and he says, 'Christ, this is bloody good for just two and six, ain't it?' The other bloke said, 'You think this is good? You should have been here last week. There was some bloke in there screwing a kangaroo.' "

Chris lit himself another cigarette. Carol was laughing. She said, "God, I wouldn't fancy it with a bloody kangaroo."

Someone said, "Well, it wouldn't be exactly the same for you as it would for that bloke."

Jacky said, "I reckon having it with a kangaroo would be bloody marvelous. Christ, think of the size of that thing you'd have moving around inside you if you were having it with a kangaroo." She pushed her hand against her skirt, laughing. "Man."

Pete looked across at Chris. "Makes ya feel you're not wanted, don't it?"

They grinned.

"How long you gonna be in Edinburgh?"

"I ain't sure. We leave tomorrow night, don't we, Chris?"

"Yeah, Deene said we go to Dunfermline tomorrow night, didn't he? Then we have a few more days back here in the middle of the tour."

Jacky said, "We was gonna come and see the show tonight, but we didn't have the money. So we went to the pictures instead."

"Where d'you live, then?"

"We're both staying at Carol's house. My parents are away on holiday."

They sat for a while and then started off toward the hotel. Chris and Carol followed after Pete and Jacky along the road. Pete turned back. "Hey, keep your eyes open. We might as well get a taxi if we can find one."

They walked for a while and found a taxi. Carol phoned her mother from outside the hotel. "Mum, we're going to a party. We'll see you in the morning."

They dodged the man on the desk at the hotel and took the elevator up to the third floor. Ray and Dave passed them as they got out of the elevator. "Hi, where's Bob Deene got to?"

"We just left him. We're turning in."

They walked through to their rooms. By the time they woke up the next morning, it was about eight o'clock. Pete and Jacky came through the connecting door to Carol and Chris, and they sat around for a while, playing their guitars and lying on the beds, sunlight filtering in through the dusty windows.

There was a letter in the post from Spud and one from Napoleon. Napoleon was living in London. Chris had met him almost a year ago. He was a hippie, an anarchist and an unpublished poet. Chris read through the letter slowly, lying on the bed. Napoleon had been a good friend. Chris wanted to see him again. He decided to see him as soon as the tour was over, as soon as he could get back to London.

Pete sat toying with his guitar. He said, "Dave couldn't get over. He's off with that bird in the pink skirt, the one he was talking to last night."

Chris said, "It doesn't matter. We can do the song tomorrow. Why don't we go for a walk around, explore Edinburgh?"

One of the girls said, "We could take you to Cramond Island. What time d'you have to be back?"

"Not till this afternoon. About three o'clock."

"We'll take ya to Cramond Island, then. It's a big island in the Firth of Forth. When the tide's in, the whole island is surrounded by the sea. And when the tide's right out, there's a pipeline with a causeway joined to it which connects the island up to the mainland. When the tide's out, you can walk across to the island and have parties there and everything. And when the tide's in, it surrounds the whole island, and no one can get near you."

"Great," Pete said. "How can we get out there?"

"You have to get a bus out of Edinburgh. Then you walk for a while."

They left the hotel and found the bus stop. Chris and Pete took their guitars with them, and they took the bus out of Edinburgh, through Leith, and then back into the outskirts of Edinburgh again. They walked to the camping site at Muirhouse and then down onto the beach. Carol pointed out toward the sea. "There y'are. Cramond Island."

The island stood out in the middle of the firth. Chris could see the blockhouses on each side of it, where it had been fortified during some forgotten war. He could see the seabirds flying to the far end of the island, the small waves breaking against the rocks.

Jacky said, "The tide's out. We should be able to get across."

They started to walk toward the pipeline. They could see it jutting out of the water, a long arm stretching out into the sea. Pete and Jacky started to walk. Chris caught up with them, pulling along Carol beside him. They all laughed and joked. The beginning of the pipeline was about a mile away, out along the beach. They walked toward it quickly. People passed them walking in the opposite direction, talking busily or looking at the sea. They got to the pipeline and started out toward the island. The pipeline was slippery, pools of water left behind on either side of it by the tide.

"Look at that. A bloody jellyfish."

"Christ, yeah. Look at the size of that fucking thing."

The jellyfish lay in a pool of water, stranded by the tide. A huge, transparent eye looked up at them from the red blob. They watched the jellyfish for a moment and then moved on.

"How the hell'd that thing get up here?"

"We get thousands of 'em. I reckon they must like it up here or something."

They reached the end of the pipeline and walked onto the causeway. The causeway was slippery, too, pools of water left on it and beds of seaweed. They slipped and splashed along the causeway until finally they got to the island. They scrambled over the large rocks embedded in the beach. The first blockhouse was set aside from the others, near to the causeway on the south side of the island. It was set on rocks high above the beach. They climbed the rocks quickly onto the grass surrounding the blockhouse. Chris stood there, leaning on his guitar and looking up at the cold stone and bricks of the blockhouse. Pete climbed the steps inside, and the others followed him. The blockhouse was divided into two rooms, one big and one small, and out where the machine guns had once been mounted, there was a large sun lounge overlooking the sea. They stood looking at the sea for a while, the sun and the wind beating against their faces. The words began to formulate in Chris' mind for a book, a song, a million poems. He stood with Carol, their shoulders touching as they watched the waves.

Pete said, "Man, this is great. You could live out here for years. No police, no one to bother you, nothing. It's marvelous."

Carol said, "You get a lot of hippies sleeping out over here. Sometimes there's parties going on all night."

Pete whistled. "Great."

They unslung their guitars and sang the song they'd been trying to write. Chris added new words and changed the song around, and they laughed and sang on. After they'd finished singing, they smoked and went to explore the rest of the island.

They found the blockhouse on the other side of the island and went inside. The walls were filled with names. Terry . . . Jim . . . Donovan Slept Here . . . Frankie . . .

Carol found some chalk, and they scrawled their names on the walls. Pete sat down on the floor on top of all the dirt and rubble while Jacky sat on his knee, and Chris and Carol climbed up onto the roof, took off their shoes and sat with their feet dangling over the edge of the blockhouse, sunbathing. They talked for a while, and then they climbed down again onto the rocks and up onto the grass. They walked to another

83

of the blockhouses and sat down on their coats inside. All the doors and windows were open, and the wind blew in, fresh and clean.

Carol undid the buttons of her blouse and lay down on the ground. Chris lay next to her. He imagined that the bomb had dropped and that the four of them were the only four people left alive in the world. He had a feeling of complete contentment, a feeling of restfulness. There was another place where he got exactly the same feeling, a small town in Spain where he had once gone with Lorraine to drink Coke and rum and to lie by the sea. Calella de la Costa, on the western Mediterranean, near to Barcelona. He rolled the names around in his mind. Cramond Island. Calella de la Costa. He felt happy, wonderful. The cigarette smoke whirled up in lazy spirals above his mind. The girl lay there next to him, groaning softly as his hands touched her. He threw away his cigarette, and they both undressed. They sat there, hardly speaking, caressing the whole of each other's bodies, moving their hands over the whole of each other's warm skins. The girl kissed him on his chest, on his stomach, on his thighs, through the pubic hair and down between his legs. He put his hands around her bent head, kissed her on her neck, ran his hands along the outline of her spine. He felt her mouth, her tongue, upon his penis, felt her hands pressed against his hips, steadying herself, her body moving softly. He felt a feeling of powerlessness, as

84

if all he could do, all he wanted to do, was to sit there. He could feel the wind on his back, the drafts blowing from window to window through the room. He ran his hands against her skin, tried to kiss her again on her neck, but couldn't reach. He sat back, threw back his head, threw himself open almost to her lips. He felt suddenly that this was the complete reversal. Instead of her opening her legs to him, it was him opening his legs to her. Instead of him working on the girl's body, it was her working on his. He could just sit there, his head thrown back, his eyes on the ceiling. He felt he could hardly move, hardly do anything.

A moment later it was over. They both flopped down on top of their coats. Carol spoke quickly. She said, "Oh, God."

"What?"

"God, it was marvelous."

"What did you feel?"

She looked over at him. "I don't know. I seemed to have an orgasm. I could feel my orgasm building up all the time I had it in my mouth. Then I could feel it jerking. I could feel the wind on me, and I could feel my orgasm building up higher and higher. Oh, God." She closed her eyes and lay back. She pulled over her blouse and wiped her neck.

They smoked for a while—Carol's cigarettes, tipped Consulate. Chris closed his eyes, too, and lay close to Carol. He drew on his cigarette.

"It's funny. It always makes me feel the same when I have it like that. It makes me feel like I'm the woman and you're the man."

"Christ. We must be queer or something."

He laughed. "Fuck off." He turned around to her and ran his fingers over her mouth. He lay back again and closed his eyes. The feeling of peace came over him again, the feeling of them being the only four people left alive in the world. He could hear the sound of the sea. As it was in the beginning, is now, and ever shall be . . . The two things that had never changed in the whole history of the world: the sound of the sea beating against the rocks and the peaceful aftermath of sex. He lay there, smoking and thinking. The time passed quickly. He felt suddenly that he wanted to stay there for the rest of the day, the rest of the month.

Carol turned over to him; they made love and then got dressed. When they went outside, the others were sitting on one of the roofs. They all walked back slowly toward the solitary blockhouse by the pipeline. They stood on the rocks and watched as the water began to wash up higher over the seaweed and concrete causeway.

Pete said, "Why don't we go back and find a café? Get something to eat."

"Yeah, I'm starving."

They climbed down again onto the beach. Jacky slipped on one of the rocks and almost fell.

They laughed. Pete said, "Hey, watch it, darling, you'll end up with a twisted womb."

They climbed over a bed of mussels, black and oily, packed together at the beginning of the causeway. Carol looked down at her laddered stockings. "Christ, I'll have to get some new stockings."

"Don't see what ya wear 'em for, anyway. Take 'em off."

She stood in one of the puddles on the causeway and took off her shoes. She handed them to Chris. "Hold my shoes, then."

He held her shoes and watched her as she took off her stockings. She laughed and put back on her shoes, tossing the stockings over her shoulder as she started to walk.

Chris looked back at Cramond Island and waved it silent good-bye.

II

The coach rolled through the roads and country lanes toward Dundee. It was almost the end of the first part of the tour. Pete sat toward the front, his feet up on the seat in front of him. Chris sat next to him by the window, sleeping. It was about five o'clock in the afternoon. The roads rolled past them endlessly, mile upon mile of grass and tar. They reached the outskirts of Dundee. Chris woke up.

"We almost there?"

"Yeah, almost." Pete moved his feet, sank lower in the chair. "You heard from Lorraine?"

"No, I haven't heard a thing."

"Where is she?"

"She's with her family. They're bastards, all of 'em. Her father's queer, and her mother's a nagging, bloody old gossip."

"You make 'em sound lovely," Pete said, laughing. "What about Lorraine, though? She's no bastard."

"No, she's no bastard, but they act like she was. She puts up with bloody near everything from them, and all she gets back in return is orders not to take me anywhere near the house in case of what the neighbors might think." Chris swore. He said, "Aw, they make me bloody sick."

Pete laughed again. "You wanna try and go back to sleep again?" he said. "You been working hard the last two weeks, and you was sitting up writing again last night. You ought to get some sleep."

Chris nodded. He looked down at the large, quarto-sized notebook resting on his lap. He had been writing in it now all through the tour, whenever there was a spare moment. It was a book, the first book he'd ever tried to write. Spud had suggested it almost four months ago. "You can't say all ya wanna say in a song. All right then, why don't you try writing prose?"

The writing had been murder. His hands and fingers

had been covered, night after night, by leaking ink. His arm had been numb from the continuous exercising of it, and his brain, early each morning when he had finished writing, was spent and exhausted.

The coach halted at a crossroads. Chris looked out around him. The weather was cold and windy. It was the middle of August. A cold wind in August. He laughed. Pete looked around at him. "What's up?"

"Oh, nothing, just thinking." He searched for his cigarettes, and the coach moved off again. They arrived at the theater and the coach drove off to their hotel, carrying their luggage.

"What ya gonna do tomorrow?" Pete said. "Dave reckoned he could give us a lift to Edinburgh in the car. The others aren't leaving till tomorrow night, but Dave wants to get there early. He's getting a train down to London."

"What you gonna do? Drive down with Dave?"

"Yeah, I thought I might as well."

"I'll come with you, then."

"I thought we could find some cheap hotel in Edinburgh. Just sleep for the next four days."

"Yeah, I could do with it." Chris grinned. "I've been having nightmares. I don't reckon I've been getting enough sleep recently."

They walked with the others along the passage toward the dressing rooms. "What sort of nightmares?"

"Oh, I don't know." Chris became serious. "The

nightmares always seem to be the same. I see the vision of something, a monster which I can't explain, always the same and yet always different. I see it in color, too— very vivid color—but usually all my dreams are in black and white. The colors seem to mean something, seem to change suddenly. And when I wake up, I feel terrified, really physically scared. I don't know how to explain it. It all seems stupid." He looked around at Pete. Pete was watching him soberly, saying nothing. He seemed to have caught the scent of how serious it all was, how important it was. They entered Chris' dressing room, stopped walking.

Chris said, "I saw this vision once before. I've only ever told one or two other people about this. It was in Spain. I was on the beach one night, just sitting there. It was the time I had that big row with Lorraine. I was just sitting on the beach—I think probably I was drunk —and coming out of the water I could see suddenly this apparition. I know now that it was just my imagination, just like seeing pink elephants, or something like that. But at the time I believed in it implicitly. I ran along the beach as fast as I could run. I must have run almost the whole length of the beach. The next morning I woke up with a hangover, half buried in the sand. I never went anywhere near that beach the whole of the next day. I don't know how to put it all into words. It just sounds ridiculous, but it was all so real to me, so concrete. And these nightmares are just the same. I wake up sweating and terrified." He looked over at the door. Pete watched his eyes. They seemed to grow larger as he concentrated on the door. His fingers moved irritably over the top of the guitar. He shook his head suddenly. "Christ, we'd better go and get something to eat, or I'll end up giving you nightmares, too."

Pete grinned sheepishly, and they found the others, unpacked their sandwiches and had something to eat. Chris ate in silence. The American, Bob Deene, talked about New York and the job he'd once had on a tour with Bob Dylan. Pete watched Chris to see what he thought of Deene's ideas on Bob Dylan, but Chris didn't even seem to be listening.

After they'd eaten, they went to inspect the stage. Dave and Pete rearranged their loudspeakers, and Deene tested the microphones and made last-minute alterations to his script as the Representative did a quick rehearsal and arranged what they would sing. Chris sat in the wings and worked on ideas for a new song.

> Your mind is spinning in wordless confusion
> And outside your body
>> the land stakes its claim
>> to your mind and your brain.
>> The wind and the rain
>> come with your pain
> And you feel you are—dying.

But don't worry
    don't worry
It's not real, it's just a void.
No one is real
Nothing is real
    It's—just a void
        —just a void. . . .

He scribbled the words down and then put a line through the page in disgust and pushed the crumpled piece of paper away into his jacket pocket. Deene came over and sat with him for a minute. Deene offered him his half-empty packet of Black Russians.

"Smoke?"

"Yeah, thanks."

Chris tried to talk. He said, "What'd ya think of Dylan's stage act, then?"

"It's a lot like yours. Very simple. Very informal too, though. If he doesn't like the audience, he swears at them. If you ask me, Dylan's either the first prophet this generation's produced or the greatest con man in the world."

Chris said, "You sound like you think he's most likely a con man."

"Well, prophets aren't that common nowadays, but there's plenty of con men."

They smoked on in silence. The others moved about in the background, talking and rehearsing. By eight o'clock it was time for the show to start. Chris would go on first, then a Glasgow group called the Men. Then the Representative, and then Chris again.

He went through his first act quickly, singing the songs without even seeming to hear what he was singing. When he was finished, he stood for a while by the side of the stage. Pete watched him as he took a small, matchbox-sized box from his pocket and swallowed a handful of pills. He'd been drugging himself now for something like ten days. Sometimes he took so many that he hardly seemed to know what he was doing. One night he had almost collapsed on the stage. A girl had shouted out at him, "Boy, you're blocked." Chris had said, "Man, when I take these things, I'm more sane than you are."

The drugs made him talk to himself, see things which weren't there. He stood alone by the side of the stage. His eyes seemed to be concentrated on the ceiling. It was as if he were in a trance.

Deene came across and stood with Pete. He followed his eyes, saw that he was watching Chris. Deene said, "That guy's got problems."

"Yeah."

He looked over at Pete. "But you can't help him, though. He's a great character, and he's gotta live his life for himself. You can't do it for him."

Deene walked away again, and Pete watched him thoughtfully. Pete's hair was shortish, short over the front, slightly longer over the ears and neck. His

93

clothes were neat and colorfully mod. He'd never really talked to Deene until now, never thought of him before as anything but a fat, thirtyish American. Pete said to himself suddenly, "At least Chris is fighting his problems. Deene hasn't got any. What about mine? So far, I've never even faced them."

Pete went onto the stage feeling frustrated, dissatisfied. At the end of the act there was an interval of fifteen minutes or so while they played records, and then Deene came back onto the stage again to introduce Chris. Chris then did another half-hour session of folk music to end the show. As soon as the interval came, Pete went to Chris' dressing room, banged on the door and went in.

Chris was sitting over in one corner.

"Hi."

"Hi. You working?"

"No, just waiting to go on. I got another fifteen minutes."

Pete sat down. He said, "What you looking for in life, Chris?"

"How d'you mean?" Chris was drugged to his eyeballs. His voice sounded really serious, as if he wanted to talk all night.

Pete said, "I don't know. Standing out there just now, I got a sudden feeling it was all a waste of time. I had a vision of all those people out there, the things they do every day, digging roads, serving behind a counter in some shop, washing floors—all of them wasting their time away, plodding along day after day with no reason behind it all. And it appears to me you've been feeling just the same thing. Only the way I see it, you know what it is you're searching for. Your only trouble is that you can't find it. My trouble is that I can't even work out what it is I'm chasing."

"If you've got nothing to search for, man, then you're lucky. You wanna go back and join the others out there before you find something. 'Cos when you find something to search for, then either you've gotta spend the rest of your life chasing it or you've gotta work out some way to actually catch it. And if you ask me, you'd be better off not even knowing it existed." Chris was quiet again. He pointed in front of him to the toilet, just off to the side of the room. "Look at that thing over there. I masturbated into that thing ten minutes ago. I flushed spunk down that pipe over there with a million tons of water. Just think what it was that flushed down that toilet, Pete. If that had landed in some girl's crutch instead of in that pipe, then in nine months' time it might have been a baby. And nineteen years after that, that baby would have been as old as you and me. And perhaps it would be sitting in here the same as we are, searching for some sort of paradise that it could probably never find, chasing after some politician's dream suspended on the far distant horizon, beating its brains out for some demi-

Eden of the clouds which doesn't even exist. I tell ya, man, it's better off as just a drop of spunk flushed down some Scottish toilet."

Chris stood up to get himself a cigarette and lurched against the table.

"You don't really believe that," Pete said.

"Why not?"

"Because if you did, you'd shoot yourself."

"Yeah, perhaps I would. But what other way is there to think?"

"I reckon you already know the other way. You know what you're looking for, don't you?"

"Yeah, I know what I'm looking for. I've said it so many times, I've got sick of hearing the sound of my own voice. I'm looking for Mr. Tambourine Man's paradise. I'm looking for the far distant horizon just like everyone else." He looked up to the mirror on the wall, with the array of electric lights reflected in it from the neon streets outside. "Look up at that thing, man. See the lights and the colors? That's what I'm searching for. Look up into it. That's paradise, man, can't you see it? Can't you see the Happy Prince wandering in the background, and the little swallow standing there with Napoleon Bonaparte? And Andrés Segovia there, with a shotgun hanging from his guitar strings, playing Bob Dylan and reading his Koran? Can't you see it all, man? Am I so mad you can't keep up with me, Pete? Or are you that mad, too? Sometimes I think going

mad would be the only way. I'm on the brink of it already; I know that. But it isn't really madness. It's
really just a deeper type of sanity. Madness isn't really
insanity at all; it's exactly the opposite. If people were
really sane, then they'd realize that the man shut up in
some lunatic asylum is the only really happy man in
the whole world. They said Dickens was mad. Pete,
did ya know that? And Nietzsche. And Nijinsky." Chris
stood up and fell again, against the table.

Pete got to his feet. "Come on, sit down. You better
have a drink."

"I'm all right. What's the matter with ya? I'll be all
right."

He flopped down in the chair again. Pete found him
a glass of water, stood over him. Chris seemed to quiet
down. He looked up suddenly into Pete's eyes. "You
know, I really saw it all just a minute ago, Pete. Looking into that mirror, I could see everything. It was nirvana, and Eden, and paradise—everything." He closed
his eyes. "I need to be able to think again, to be able to
work out what things mean and what I'm doing here.
My mind is just a desert. Nothing seems to grow there
anymore. The ground is barren and useless, and all I
ever see is mirages and shifting clouds of sand which
just confuse me and don't mean anything. I want to
stop the world spinning for a while, slow it all down so
that I have a chance to look at it all, a chance to work
out what's happening. . . .

97

"Once, when I was young, I used to believe in God and in religion and in all the trappings and legends of it. And I used to think that somehow, deep down inside myself, there was something different about me. I had this feeling when I saw other people that they were in some way *outside* me, and I was *inside*. I looked at this body which is growing around me, and I realized that this body, this combination of flesh and bone and so many pints of blood—all this wasn't me at all. I was inside it. I realized that bodies didn't make up people at all. It was something inside, a sort of soul. And my particular soul—the thing that was doing my thinking and my reasoning and my wondering for me—was somehow different, somehow special. I used to think that in some way I might be God without even realizing it. Didn't you ever wonder about that? The possibility that perhaps this person, God, this great idol that the world got down on its knees to prostitute itself before, was really you? The idea always fascinated me. This feeling of being something inside, of being something special, just made it all seem more possible, more likely. Even though really I knew it was all stupid.

"And now I have this feeling of specialness inside me again. I think that everyone must have it. Some people don't notice it, perhaps, or they're able to dismiss it in some way, so they don't have to worry about it, but I'm sure that it's present in everyone. And everyone has to do something to fulfill this feeling. Everyone must work first of all on his own salvation. Of course, though, if you're one of the people who doesn't even recognize this feeling inside himself, then you've got nothing to worry about. You're on top of the world, man. You can go out and get drunk every night, spend all your days lying in bed, smoking hash. What does it matter? What does it matter even if you do recognize the feeling? You can't do anything about it. If anyone had ever succeeded in finding paradise, then he really would have become God. And no one has yet, so you might just as well give up and try to enjoy yourself."

Chris looked up at the clock. He said, "Man, I better get on-stage." He staggered up and made toward the door. Pete followed him.

"Christ, I feel high. My head feels like it's in space."

Pete said, "Perhaps you better not go on."

"Don't worry about me. I'll be all right." They reached the side of the stage. Chris said, "Man, I'm gonna give the longest version of 'Tambourine Man' they ever heard."

Deene stood with them as he waited to do the introductions. He said to Chris, "There was a guy here to see ya. A weird guy. Didn't drink, didn't smoke, didn't even breathe. He said his name was Olson. Said he met you at Brighton, and he'd been watching you. I asked him if he wanted to wait, but he said no. He said it was too late, and if he couldn't see ya now, there was nothing he could do."

"Olson? Christ, he's some kind of nut. How the hell'd he know where I was?"

Deene shrugged. He watched Chris' eyes. "You sure you wanna go on? Sure you feel up to it?"

"Yeah, sure. Don't go out and introduce me. I'll go on the stage by myself." He threw away his cigarette, and as the curtain went up, he walked out with his guitar onto the bare stage.

III

Chris woke up with a hangover. He hadn't been drinking at all, but he felt he'd swallowed all the beer in the world. Pete was doing some packing.

Chris struggled out of bed. He said, "Christ, Pete, what the hell happened last night?"

"How d'you mean?"

"I remember sitting in that bloody dressing room and talking and talking like some sort of lecturer at Oxford University. Then when I got to bed, I had a dream about some crank called Olson, who I met once at Brighton. Why the hell should I dream about him?"

"Don't you remember him coming to see ya last night?"

"Olson?"

"Yeah, he wanted to see you. Deene said he'd better wait till after the show, and Olson said he couldn't wait that long and went away."

Chris held his head. "God, I don't remember any of that." He stretched his arms and shook his head. They packed quickly, and an hour later they were in the car with Dave, driving to Edinburgh. Chris sat with his guitar in the back. Scotland passed by them outside the windows. It looked to Chris almost exactly as he had always imagined Scotland should look. For a while the road ran alongside a railway line, and Chris had visions of Benjamin Disraeli, coughing and spluttering in his usual abnormal ill-health as he traveled up on the train from London to visit the queen on her estates in Scotland and to tell her that he'd just bought the Suez Canal. "I knew it was your birthday coming up, Victoria my dear, so I borrowed the odd four million pounds from my good friends the Rothschilds and got you a little present."

Chris closed his eyes and fell asleep. At Edinburgh they booked into a hotel, and Dave left the car with Pete and went to catch the train down to London.

Chris and Pete sat in the hotel room, listening to Pete's collection of records. Chris brought out the book he was trying to write. He hadn't decided yet what the book should be called. He wrote out some of the titles he'd thought of onto a single sheet of paper. Pete watched him as he crossed off some of the titles, changed others. Finally he was left with just one. *A Drum for Dave Moselle.* He repeated the title over and over to himself beneath his breath. The title was quite good. He liked it. He pushed the book aside and sat back in his chair.

They listened to the records and began to talk.

"You remember when we were in Edinburgh a couple of weeks ago? Going over to Cramond Island?"

"Yeah, that place was great, weren't it?"

"Yeah, great. The sort of place you could live cut off from everyone. No one to talk to ya, no one to bother you, just you and the sea and the island."

Pete looked over at him. "You're getting very solitary lately, ain't ya?"

"Yeah, I s'pose I am. It's being up here in Scotland for two weeks, away from Lorraine and everything. I don't know. It's strange. I don't know what I said last night, but I get these periods when I feel just cut off from everything. I feel alone, depressed, almost as if I'm another person. And if someone else happens to be around me, the way you were last night, then they just get engulfed by me in a wave of all my verbal wanderings. You must've been bored stiff."

"I was trying to find out what you were thinking about, Chris. You know, trying to find out what your answer to it all was." Pete looked serious. He smiled suddenly. "Oh, God. Why don't we have a party or something, forget about it all?"

"Yeah, great."

"We can phone up those two birds we met before, two weeks ago, get them to bring some of their friends along, perhaps. We could have the party out on Cramond Island."

Chris sat up. "Yeah, that's marvelous. You do the phoning. Tell everyone to bring along a bottle. And I'll go out and get some wine and some fags."

He went out into the streets and hunted for the wine. Walking through the crowded streets gave him a feeling of excitement, intense happiness. It was dinner time, and he went into a pub, bought three bottles of wine— two red and one white—and a bottle of cider. He walked on for a while, just for the fun of walking, and finally bought himself a loaf of fresh-baked bread and ripped it in half to eat it, eating as he walked back toward the hotel.

About three o'clock that afternoon they drove out to Cramond Island, sat in the car for a while, waiting for the tide to go out, and then crossed over on the pipeline and got onto the island. Everything looked exactly as it had done the time before. They left the bottles up in the first blockhouse with their guitars and went down onto the beach to light a fire. Chris collected together the wood while Pete burned some straw to start the flame. When the fire was finally alight, they sat around it on the rocks and watched it burn. They tried to calculate how long it would be before the tide came in again, but finally they gave up. They smoked their cigarettes and joked with each other until almost seven o'clock. The fire was down to just a few embers now, and they left it to go out and climbed back to the blockhouse.

A group of hazy figures were coming across to them from the other end of the pipeline. Chris and Pete watched them from the machine-gun bay facing down onto the sea. When they got nearer, they could see Jacky and Carol and five others, two girls and three boys. One of the boys carried a guitar. They climbed up the rocks and onto the old machine-gun emplacement. Jacky saw Pete and Chris, yelled, and then ran up to them and kissed them both. Chris picked her up, and they held her between them and pretended to throw her down onto the rocks by the sea.

Jacky introduced them to all the others. The tallest of the other girls was called Took. The other one's name Chris didn't quite catch, but the boy she was with was called Jim. The remaining two boys' names were lost amid the general chatter and excitement. The boy with the guitar immediately began to examine Pete's guitar. "Christ, these things cost about ninety quid."

His own guitar was almost the same as the one Chris used. They began opening their bottles immediately and climbed down onto the beach to get some wood for a new fire out on the balcony.

It was just past half past eight, and far off in the distance the red sun sank gradually upon the blue waters, and it started slowly to get dark. Chris found himself on the beach next to Carol. So far he'd hardly spoken to her. He grinned. "How ya doing?"

She sounded quiet when she answered. "I'm all right," she said.

Chris didn't seem even to notice, and they climbed to the blockhouse with him talking to her madly. When they got inside, the first flames of the fire were already flickering against the cold brick wall. The fire was situated in the corner of two walls, shielded from the wind. The wind blowing off the sea was really strong, breathtaking, and the smoke from the fire blew out straight onto the still rocks as soon as it caught the wind.

The boy with the guitar stood strumming on it before the fire and talking to Pete at the same time. The mixed, confused conversations rang out loudly against the surrounding brick walls. "We got a truck all the way down to London. We got to Cornwall in about three days."

"What's happened to the rest of the wine?"

"We thought you'd be coming back last week. How was the tour?"

Chris got into an argument with Jim over the symbolism of "The Gates of Eden" and personalized religion. Jim was a poet and read some of his poetry into the wind, choking as he did so from the smoke of the fire. Pete got the guitar player to play "Catch the Wind" and "Mr. Tambourine Man," and they discussed their favorite folk music to the background of Jim's poetry.

Chris talked to Jim about the book he was trying to write and about the impossibility of publishing poetry anywhere outside America. The whole affair was wild and irrepressible. It was like something from a book by Jack Kerouac or from the letters of Sue Cohen. Carol stood in the background. At one point Chris went over to her, and they stood by the fire in silence, smoking. Chris guessed that she was upset about something, but every time he asked her what it was, she just shook her head and tried to laugh. In the end he dismissed it, and they danced around the logs of wood stacked up for the fire, and Carol seemed to snap out of it. She told him how she hadn't been able to get any of her favorite cigarettes (menthol), and he showed her some of his book (which she was very interested in and which no one except Pete had ever read before), and she said it was crazy and all very sad, and then they went back to the edge of the balcony and sat on the blockhouse floor.

Chris looked over at Took and Took looked down at him, and he decided that he'd like to go to bed with her. Then he laughed to himself at how happy he was and how unhappy he'd been up until just a few hours ago, and how narrow the tightrope seemed to be between happiness and depression; then he thought how immoral it was to sit there with Carol and to think about going to bed with Took, and he laughed. Then after a while someone threw his guitar over at him, and he and Pete played the song that they'd written together two and a half weeks before.

When it was over he sat back on the floor again, and Took stayed where she was, sitting on the wall with her legs dangling down toward the floor and brushing against his shoulder. Carol passed him the wine and told him to give her a cigarette, and he gave her one and closed his eyes against the smoke; he was so happy at that moment that he fell almost instantly into the shortest sleep of his life. When he woke up again, hardly any time had passed at all, and he imagined the whole history of the island in the flashing of just a couple of seconds. He imagined the deserted, crumbling houses right in the center of the island, imagined them when they had been lived in and when the rain had lashed at them in the middle of the winter back in the years before he, before his mother, before his grandmother, before even her grandmother had been born. He imagined the summer of 1963 or 1964, when Donovan with his entourage had come to the island to write his poetry and his songs which in the spring of 1965 would make him a household name. He imagined Philip Binner, the innocent poet from Yorkshire, who had come to Edinburgh for the festival in 1966 and who had left his name with the million others on the yellow, moldering blockhouse walls. He looked around at Carol, found the wine again and took another drink. Took allowed herself to be dragged off into the corner to be kissed and to light a cigarette in the shelter, away from the wind. Chris watched her as she walked back again to sit down. She reminded him of his hippie from Folkestone beach, July-Anne. She held her newly lit cigarette between her fingers delicately. Her hair flopped over her shoulders like the pitch-black mane of an Arabian stallion. He wondered what other comparisons there were that he could think of for her. Carol disappeared to get some more wood with Pete and Jacky. Chris talked for a while to Took.

"What do you do? Write or paint?"

"Oh, I don't do anything. I just sit around and watch."

They opened another bottle of wine and drank it dry. Chris stood up for a moment and threw the empty bottle away, down onto the rocks by the sea. The crash of the breaking glass was soft in the now dark night. The tide was coming back in, the first tentative waves beginning to wash against the pipeline. Chris watched it all, the beauty of it, the dark, mysterious, hidden power driving those waves forward, so dangerous and so beautiful. He felt that he didn't care what he said anymore, what he said or even what he thought. As long as this party went on, he felt he would be happy. It had turned into the best party he had had in months, the best in years. Why should life have a plot or a reason behind it? Life was like a book. Why should a book have a plot to it? The fact that things happened, that was enough. He stood there, all his thoughts merged into one, everything contracted together into the dead fag end which he held in his hand, the dead fag end which epitomized to him suddenly the entirety of life.

The boy with the guitar began to play "Mr. Tambourine Man" again. Chris sat and listened to it all, silent. He closed his eyes, allowed himself to be lulled, mesmerized. It seemed to be a year, an age, before it was over. Then he opened his eyes again and looked back up at Took. She said, "You want another drink?"

"Yeah, thanks."

"How'd you meet Carol?"

"We met each other in Edinburgh, when we were here on the first part of the tour. 'Bout two and a half weeks ago."

"You should meet her parents," Took said. "Bastards."

"Parents, parents. All girls' parents are bastards. I only ever met one girl's who weren't. And her parents just sat in the background all the time I was there and never said a thing."

"I reckon that's the best kind."

"Yeah, I s'pose it is."

The others returned, and Pete began trying to get himself drunk on the remains of the wine. Jim and his girl sat near to the fire, and Pete went over to sit with them, all three of them exchanging poetry and attempting to do some writing by the light of the burning wood. The boy with the guitar continued with his playing—ancient Bob Dylan tunes and some touches of Paul Simon. He was really better on his guitar than both Pete and Chris put together. Each time he finished a song, he said to Chris, "Why don't you play something now?" and Chris said, "Man, if I was as good as you, I would."

"Aw, but I keep forgetting the words."

"What does that matter? Only a machine remembers all the words."

Jacky laughed. She lit a cigarette. As the time passed, it grew gradually darker, and the lazy tide came in slowly, farther and farther around the slippery pipeline. The last part of the party was played out in two distinct groups on either side of the balcony. Over by the fire, running out into the wind every so often to escape from the fumes, were Pete and Carol and the two poets. On the other side of the balcony stood all the others, colder but free from the smoke. Chris sat listening most of the time in between the two groups, listening to the conversations, watching the girls, smoking his cigarettes and occasionally drinking. When the tide had come in again almost over the pipeline, at the very last moment when it was possible to cross back to the mainland, the party broke up. Jim and his girl friend decided to stay the night and to leave in the morning with the next tide. Jacky and Carol had decided to stay too, sleeping the night with Chris and Pete in the larger of the two rooms of the blockhouse.

They said their good-byes out on the balcony. Took went over to Pete to say good-bye. He kissed her. Chris got up from where he'd been sitting and kissed her, too. He felt he should have talked to her more, found out where he could contact her, perhaps. But it was all too late. They made some final joke, and he waved his farewell to them all as the three figures made their way down from the rocks and onto the causeway, the guitar silhouetted for a moment against the paler black of the sea.

The fire had almost died down again, and they threw more wood onto it and waited for it to burn. Chris stood with Carol again. They smoked for a while, and then Chris decided to go for more wood, and Carol followed him. They climbed in silence down onto the beach. Chris noticed how quiet she was again. He said, "You been bloody quiet all evening. What's the matter with you?"

"I've been waiting to talk to you."

"What about?"

"I think I might be pregnant."

He stopped walking. "Oh, fucking hell. You can't be sure? Not yet?"

"I'm not certain. But I'm a week late. I'm probably pregnant."

"Who've you told?"

"No one." She tossed her head, looked away out to sea. "If I am, I want to have an abortion. I thought probably—you know, I thought probably you'd know someone."

"Aw, don't be a fool. You'd kill yourself."

"What d'you mean?" She turned back to face him.

"It's too bloody dangerous. It's not worth it."

The wind came at them from the north, blowing at their clothes, tearing their words from them across the beach and down toward the sea.

She said, "What d'you think I should do? I could never stay at home. If I told them, they'd kill me."

"What are they like?"

She made an expression of disgust. "I hate them." She said it without any feeling at all. Chris put his arm around her suddenly, saying nothing. She made to bend down over a group of sticks.

"Oh, leave them. Come on, we'd better walk. Let's go to the other side of the island." He lit a couple of cigarettes, gave one to her. They started off on the road, the narrow track which wound its way around to the other side of the island. Chris said, "How old are you really? Fifteen?"

"I'm sixteen next week." She drew on her cigarette. She said, "I won't tell anyone that it's yours. I mean, they could get the police after you on account of me being under sixteen. I won't say anything."

"I'm not worried about that. You can say what you fucking well like." He was dead serious. He said, "Only for God's sake, don't try and get yourself an abortion. You'll get rid of the kid, but you'd probably get rid of yourself, too."

"I want to leave home." She said it as if it were the most important part of the whole discussion, the answer to everything.

"Would they let ya go?"

"I wouldn't tell them."

They walked until they reached the other side of the island, and then they sat down, freezing, on the grass. Chris' mind was a complete blank.

"I wish I hadn't told you," Carol said.

"What d'you mean?"

"Well, it isn't your fault. It's hardly got anything to do with you. You didn't rape me or anything. I knew I was gonna go to bed with you as soon as I met you."

"So? What difference does that make? I'd still feel like trying to stop you getting an abortion and killing yourself, even if it was someone else you'd been to bed with. Why shouldn't you have told me?"

She bent her head down toward the grass. "You've got your own problems, I suppose."

"Huh." He wanted to laugh and then cry. Why the hell couldn't he have been a bit more careful? He was so senseless all the time, so thoughtless. "If nothing happens, you'd better go to a doctor," he said.

"I think I'm gonna leave home."

"Where you gonna stay?"

"I don't know."

"They could get the police to try and find you." She looked up. "D'you think they would? Be able to find me, I mean."

"They'd find you if you stayed in Edinburgh." He looked out at the sea, tossed back his long hair from out of his eyes. "Do you wanna go down to London?"

"How d'you mean?"

"Lorraine's got a flat there. Just a couple of rooms. You could stay there for a few weeks while you were getting to know your way around. Lorraine wouldn't mind. She's not even there at the moment, anyway."

"You sure she wouldn't mind?"

"We have people dropping in for a few weeks all the time. It wouldn't matter. Lorraine doesn't care."

"I don't know whether I ought to or not."

"Well, make up your own mind. Just do what you want to do. Don't do anything because someone else thinks it's the right thing to do, or you'll end up in a terrible bloody mess."

"You think perhaps I'm too young to leave home?"

"In a way you are, I s'pose. In a way I am myself. But I left home over three years ago." He swore. "Oh, it's not a question of whether you're too young or not. It's a question of whether you really want to or not. Whether you just think you want to. You can never ask anyone else whether they think you ought to do something. The only person who knows that is yourself. If you really want to leave home, then you should do it. I think probably it'd be the best thing for you."

"I could have the baby adopted."

He said, "Yeah." They got up and walked farther toward the edge of the rocks. Chris was quiet, and they stood there in silence.

Finally she said, "Can I really stay at this flat in London? You're serious about it?"

"Yeah, of course I am."

She didn't say anything for a while. He said, "I'll give you the address. If you wanna go, you can, but don't rush into it. Work out what you wanna do first."

"I think I'm gonna come," she said. She turned around, shivering suddenly. "Let's go back to the fire." She laughed.

"I wanna stand here for a while. I'll come up in a minute and bring some wood with me."

He lit a cigarette and gave her the rest of the packet to take back with her. He watched her walking back along the road until eventually she disappeared out of sight. Suddenly he felt despair again. He wanted to get away from everything, snap himself out of it. Everything seemed to have started to go wrong again suddenly. Oh, fuck everything. He felt like jumping off the rocks, drowning himself in the friendly sea, escaping from it all, never having to worry about any of it again. . . . The idea twisted itself in his mind. He'd never wanted to commit suicide so much in all his life. Why not? Why the hell shouldn't he kill himself? What was death, anyway? If death was anything, then it was heaven, if not, it was just an obscurity. So if death was heaven, what was life? If death was heaven, then life must be hell.

He edged nearer toward the rocks. But they weren't high enough. The fall wouldn't be enough to kill him, just to maim him, probably to make him a cripple for the rest of his life; and what about the chances of drowning? If he jumped, he would just land on the rocks, nowhere near the sea at all. He couldn't kill himself if he wanted to.

He stood there for almost five minutes. He wanted to see Lorraine suddenly, hitchhike all the way down to Stevenage, and then, when he got there, drag her down to London with him and have a few days in the flat again. He wanted to go now, right away, get out onto the road and forget everything.

He said suddenly, "Why not?" The sound of his own voice seemed to surprise him. He could go in the morning if he wanted to. He had a few spare days in Edinburgh. He could do what he wanted. Start hitchhiking as soon as the first tide tomorrow, take his guitar with him and play it by the side of the road as he waited for a lift.

Chris felt happy for a moment, desperately depressed

and desperately happy both at the same time. He undid
the zip of his jeans, stood and urinated over the rock
wall, against the wind, and then made his way back
slowly to the narrow road.

IV

Lorraine sat on the floor in front of the television set,
smoking. Her father sat in the armchair on the other
side of the room. It was about half past seven. The door
opened and Sidney came in, Lorraine's brother. His
father said, "Go and make a cup of tea, Sidney."

Sidney walked through to the kitchen, saying nothing. He put the kettle on and returned to the front
room again. He said, "The washing up's not done yet,
Lorraine."

She sat there without hearing. Her father said, "Lorraine, the washing up." He looked down at her, the
Victorian tyrant.

She said, "Oh, wait a minute. I'll do it later."

"Do it now." He looked at her as if it were the most
important thing in the whole world. She looked back
into his face. She thought to herself, Why the bloody
hell did I come and see them in the first place?

She walked out into the kitchen. Her mother came
through and went into the front room. She heard the
sound of her sitting down, imagined the two of them
together in there, both of them almost unaware that

the other person existed. Then she heard Sidney banging around in the corridor, picking up his things and starting to go upstairs. She heard the bangs as he climbed above her, walking overhead. He sat down in his room, began to play on his recorder, Lorraine listened for a moment to the terrible, high-pitched notes.

She tossed away her cigarette and looked down at the filthy dishes lying in the water. "Oh, my God." She said the words out loud. She dug into her pocket and lit herself another cigarette.

Halfway through the washing up, there was a knock on the door. Lorraine carried on with what she was doing. Her mother called out, "Lorraine, come here."

She went through into the front room.

"What?"

Her father pointed out through the window. He said, "I've told you before. That boy's not to come here."

"Well, who the hell is it, then?" Lorraine moved over to the window to see who it was.

When she opened the door, Chris was standing there with his guitar in his hand, his jeans and coat covered in mud and dust. She threw her arms around him. He ran his hand down against her jeans and pressed against her crutch. "Christ, give us a drink of water," he said. They walked back toward the kitchen, avoiding the front room. He said, "I bet them bastards were glad to see me."

"Oh, yeah. Bloody thrilled." She talked softly, so they wouldn't hear her. "The fucking sods."

They went into the kitchen. "What you doing here, anyway? You look terrible."

"I wanted to get away for a little while. I had a few days off, anyway. I hitchhiked down here. It helps me when I wanna stop myself from thinking too much."

"When you gotta go back?"

"Two days."

He sat on the washing machine, and she stood in front of him. She said, "Get me out of this place tonight, will ya?"

"Yeah, all right. We'll go down Bowes Lyon House. What ya gonna tell them?" He nodded toward the front room.

"Aw, fuck them."

They caught the bus to the town center and joined the crowds of crew-cutted mods in their gaily colored hipsters on their way to Bowes Lyon House. They went in, and the girl selling tickets said, "Hi. You're Chris Plater, aren't you?" and Chris said, "Yeah." The girl asked him for his autograph, and he gave it to her, and then they went in.

They went upstairs to the coffee bar. Music was pumped out at them from the loudspeaker fitted to the wall. It was a Bob Dylan song sung by Manfred Mann. Lorraine said, "Christ, that fucking song. They oughta shoot Manfred Mann for doing that to Bob Dylan."

They bought Coca-Cola and coffee and went to sit down. Chris always had a feeling of excitement when he sat in a place like this. There was a feeling of being for once exclusively with people of his own age, free from people like Lorraine's parents who hated him so much because of his long hair, free from the vicars and the priests who were so clever about him while they were standing in the protective reassurance of their pulpits, free from the old women who advocated bringing back the birch and hated him on sight just because he looked so scruffy to them, and wild, and outlandish, and young. He looked around him at the girls with their short dresses, their tight jeans, at the boys with their young smiles, their red, green, yellow-colored shirts, and yet he didn't see any of them. All he could see was the people like Lorraine's parents, probably like Carol's parents up in Edinburgh. He felt a sort of tragedy somehow, the aftereffects of Lorraine's father. The man depressed him, seemed to trigger off again all the feelings of hatred that he felt, all those feelings of sickness and desperation.

Lorraine said suddenly, "You going to London?"

"Yeah. I want you to come with me."

"Why did you come down? The real reason, I mean."

"I don't know."

"I think you're ill." She looked seriously at him.

"I'm not ill. I'm a depressive with too much imagination." He picked up his Coca-Cola and laughed at her.

She said, "I've been thinking about you. Spud was down for a couple of days, and we were talking about Brighton. I'm serious, Chris. I don't know anything about these things. Neither do you. We ain't bloody psychologists or anything. But sometimes there's something strange about you, Chris. You try to tell me about it, and you try to explain yourself to me, and while you're talking, then I understand and I know what it is you mean. But sometimes . . . I don't know. Lately the way you've talked has been really frightening. And you've talked as if it wasn't only me who was terrified, but you were frightened by everything you were talking about, too. Like when we were in Brighton. And do you remember the other time, when we were in St. Ives? You saw a vision, Chris. You seemed to imagine something, some kind of hallucination. And even when you realized it had just been a hallucination, even when we went back to the caravans and met Spud and the others, and you were lying in bed, telling jokes about it, even then you were still somehow hypnotized by what you'd seen. You were still somehow prepared to believe it was real. That's the sort of thing I'm talking about, Chris. Why can't you let us help you more with these things?"

Chris said, "My Christ, anyone who offers to just wave a magic wand and make me sane again can help me anytime he likes. But things just aren't like that." He took a drink of his Coke again. He looked over at her and saw how seriously she was watching him. He said, "Look, I'll tell you how I decided to come down here. The first time I was in Edinburgh, three weeks ago, right at the start of the tour. I was just walking around the streets with Pete Stewart." He was talking quietly, trying to explain himself to her.

"We met a couple of girls called Carol and Jacky. We took them back to the hotel with us for the night, and then the next morning they said they'd show us around Edinburgh, and they took us to this marvelous little island in the Firth of Forth called Cramond Island.

"Anyway, when we got back into Edinburgh a few days ago, halfway through the tour, we decided to phone these two birds up again and have a party on Cramond Island. So Jacky phoned around some of her friends, telling them there was gonna be a party, and they could all come along if they wanted to, etcetera, etcetera, and in the end we had this little party on the island inside one of the old blockhouses." Chris tried to explain how the party had affected him, how good it had made him feel.

"Then in the end, this party started to split up. Six of us decided to stay the night on the island, and the others left. I went down onto the beach with Carol to get some wood. Then she told me she was pregnant."

"You mean pregnant by you?"

"Yes. It was all sickening. I felt terrible. Why the hell couldn't I have bought a packet of skins or something? It wouldn't have made any difference to me. And now, just because I'd been too busy to bother taking any precautions, the poor girl was pregnant. It made all the excitement and happiness of the party just vanish. I had this feeling again of wanting to get away, of wanting to try and escape from everything." He paused for a minute.

"Anyway, the girl's parents are terrible to her. She thinks she probably wants to leave home. I told her if she wants to, she can stay with us at the flat for a few weeks until she can find somewhere to live. After we'd done all this bloody talking and working things out, I just got this sudden idea that I wanted to come down here and see you, probably go down to London."

"We could probably go down tonight," Lorraine said distantly. She talked as if she wasn't really concentrating.

"What about your parents?"

"Oh, it doesn't matter about them. They're getting sick of me, anyway. I can phone up the woman next door. She'll go and tell them I won't be in tonight. I can go to London for two days and then come back up here. How d'you think you'll get back to Edinburgh?"

"I don't know. I don't want to hitchhike again. I won't have time, not if I'm going to be in London for two days. I s'pose I'll probably have to go by train. Anyway, it doesn't matter. I'll worry about it when the time comes."

"Perhaps we ought to find out when the last train goes tonight to London."

"There's one sometime after ten o'clock. I remember it. Anyway, if we miss the train, we could try and get a lift down from someone. It's not important how we get there."

Chris felt that they'd gotten off the subject. He wanted to talk about Edinburgh again, about Pete, about Deene, about Carol, about himself. He wanted to tell Lorraine about the island. That was the most important thing to him, to explain about the island, explain to her how marvelous it was, explain how he felt about it, how solitary it was, peaceful, natural, restful. He decided he wanted another drink. They had more Coca-Cola and coffee and got themselves something to eat as well. Chris lit a couple of cigarettes. He had a sudden memory of how broke he'd once been, how he'd had to ration himself once on how many cigarettes he could afford to buy.

Lorraine said, "Perhaps it'd be better if you didn't work so hard. Perhaps you oughta take a long holiday or something."

"How d'you mean?"

"Well, perhaps it's all this rushing around the country, all the crowds and the bustle, all the noise and the one-night stands that're making you so tired. Perhaps you're living life at too fast a rate."

"Aw, you know it's nothing like that. People always like to think that folk singers and pop stars, etcetera, are all very discontented and lead lives that are really very false and empty. But it's not really true, not as far as I'm concerned, anyway. I know damn well that if I was doing any other job or living any other kind of life, then I'd be a damn sight more fed up and more depressed than ever. It's me that regulates how I react to things and whether I'm happy or not. It's the way I am, the way I've been made, not the sort of life I lead."

Lorraine said nothing. They smoked their cigarettes and stayed quiet. The pop records continued nonstop. Chris said, "You don't need to go home and get anything before we leave tonight?"

"No, I don't think so." They stayed for another half hour and then went to the telephone boxes in the town center. Chris stood outside. He watched her phoning and laughed to himself as he heard what she was saying through the closed door. She came out, and they walked to the bus stop. Lorraine said, "The woman next door thought I'd been run over. Silly cow asked me what hospital I was in."

They got to the station and onto the train and stretched out on the two long benches. Apart from Lorraine and Chris, the compartment was empty. Chris told Lorraine about the party and about the old blockhouse on Cramond Island. She imagined the whole picture in her mind. When they got to London, it was quite late. They caught the tube at King's Cross, down into Chelsea. The flat was dirty and old, situated in hippie and artist territory. Spud had found it for them. On occasions he lived there himself.

Lorraine turned on the passage light and tried to unlock the door. She said, "Spud sent us postcards from America."

He laughed. "Greenwich Village?"

"Yeah. He's found a girl who wants to paint his picture. He reckons she's got a friend who wants to paint you, too." She opened the door and turned on the light. The light flickered for a moment and then came on. "There's one of the postcards there. Look." She pointed. "Read it. The girl seems to think she's gonna paint him naked, lying in the middle of Fifth Avenue."

Chris laughed. He looked around him in the room and then closed the door.

V

In the morning they woke at nine o'clock, looked up at the sunlight streaming through the filthy, drawn curtains, and went back to sleep again for another hour. At ten o'clock Lorraine crawled out of the bed and made some coffee. They drank it sitting up in bed, yawning and blinking still at the strength of the sun.

Chris said, "Hey, you remember Olson? That nut we met in Brighton?"

"Yeah, what about him?"

"He came to see me up in Edinburgh. Bob Deene said he'd better wait—Deene's the disc jockey—and Olson told him he didn't have time to wait. He'd have to go."

"My God."

"What?"

"Well, he came to see me, too. He's an absolute maniac. He seemed to think we were in need of spiritual help. He kept talking about saving us and our impending doom. He was really cracked. And those eyes. Christ, I don't know how the hell he does it. They look so real and frightening, but the color of them—that sort of red color. It's impossible."

Chris sipped at his hot black coffee. He gulped a bit too much of it, and the coffee was so hot that it burned his tongue and the back of his throat. He shivered and pulled the blanket up around his shoulders to try to keep warm. Lorraine took the coffee and drank some of it herself. They had only one plastic cup in the whole flat. Chris stretched out for his cigarettes and lit one. They shared the fag between them, too.

"Where did Olson find you?" Chris said.

"At home. He just seemed to turn up out of the blue. God knows how he got the address. He came one day when there was no one else at home. He was just like you imagine Luther or somebody would be. 'Soon it will be too late,' he kept saying. It was as if he imagined he was about to destroy the whole world, and he thought it was his duty to prepare people, to gather the faithful around him."

Chris grinned. "I want to see Napoleon sometime," he said. "He wrote to me in Scotland. Spud sent a letter, too. I'd almost forgotten about it. Nap's living in Putney somewhere. I want to try and find him again."

Lorraine was lying down again, her arms stretched out now across his naked legs beneath the blanket. "What you gonna do about having a holiday?" she said.

"Oh, I don't know." He looked down at her. "I'll take some time off after this tour. I want to do some writing. I've got a few ideas for songs. They need concentrating on, though. And I want to finish that book off. The bloody thing's such fucking hard work. I should have finished it already. If it's still not done by the end of the tour, then I'll finish it off then."

He gave her the cigarette, and she drew on it for a moment and gave it back to him. She closed her eyes and said, "Wake me up in about half an hour."

At about twelve o'clock they got up out of bed and went to Putney. They strolled hand in hand along the streets. The shops and the traffic, the cars and the people, everything looked busy. They stopped outside an old surplus supplies shop. Chris said, "I wanna buy myself a parka."

"What the hell for?"

"I've been meaning to for weeks. Thinking about Napoleon just reminded me of it."

Chris went into the shop, bought the parka, and then they carried on. The place where Napoleon was living was just one big house converted into rooms. They pressed Napoleon's bell on the door downstairs, but there was no answer. They pushed open the front door, climbed up the stairs, found Napoleon's room, and banged hard on the door. A voice said, "Who the fucking hell is it?"

"Hi ya, Nap, it's us."

The door swung open.

"Chris, it's you. Come on in. We'll have a party. Napoleon jumped back over the bed and turned off the record player. He said, "I heard the bell ringing, but I didn't answer it. All the kids are on holiday from school. They walk along the streets, pressing all the bloody doorbells." He stretched out his hand and said, "How ya doing, then?"

"Great. We just arrived down here last night. I been on tour with Pete. He said he'd seen ya in London a few weeks ago."

Nap went over to the kettle on top of the gas ring. He said, "I'll make some coffee. There's no chairs. You better sit down on the bed or something. Christ, it must be months since the last time I saw ya. I been down to Brighton. I met this Swedish girl there. Her old man was a millionaire or something. She wanted me to go and live with her in Sweden. Christ, that girl's mind was really in a mess. She went around telling people we were in love with each other. Everyone thought we were going to Stockholm together. I had to pack me things and get up to London again quick. She was all right, man, but too serious. You would've thought I'd proposed to her or something."

He put the water on for the coffee. Napoleon sat on the floor while Chris and Lorraine sat on the bed. They talked on, through the coffee, through the toast which followed it, and through the second course of coffee. Chris lay out on the bed on his stomach, with his feet swinging in the air behind him. Napoleon talked madly about every subject under the sun. It made Chris feel really happy again to hear Napoleon talking. Nap was just about the most eccentric, most striking, most solid, most unchangeable person Chris had ever met. He always reminded Chris of Japhy in Kerouac's *Dharma Bums*. When Napoleon talked, you got the feeling that everything he was saying he meant and felt intensely. You got the feeling that he would still speak the same way, still swear, blaspheme and say exactly what he felt, even if he were talking to God. Napoleon was like Spud, Pete, like Chris himself. He was somehow typical of the new generation. He was the child of the 1960's, walking on two feet. He was like Dave Moselle, the hero in Chris' book. Chris smiled to himself as he thought of the idea. He'd never consciously thought of it before. He'd left the manuscript in Chelsea. It was getting bulky now. He'd show it to Napoleon sometime.

Chris said, "I been writing a book. I wanna show it to you sometime. It's about this boy who gets put into prison for refusing to be conscripted into the army."

"How long you been writing that?"

"Aw, about three weeks. I'm not sure how long exactly. I've been thinking about it for a long time. It was Spud's idea, really. He said he thought I ought to try writing something in prose."

Chris told them briefly the story of the book. Nap handed around a crumpled packet of cigarettes, and they smoked as they talked. Napoleon thought it was all marvelous and talked for a while about his own attempts at writing. Chris thought that Napoleon's poetry was the best he had ever heard. Nap was unenthusiastic about it. He always said, "Aw, anyone can write poetry like this. No poetry's worth listening to today. All the great poems have already been written, and all the great poets are dead. And even some of them were just sentimentalized lumps of nothingness."

Chris got Nap to read some of his poems, and Nap lay on the floor and read them with his cigarette in his mouth and a slice of unbuttered bread in his left hand. They all sat in relative silence for a while, eating bread, and then Nap read more poems.

About seven o'clock that evening they saw a girl come up the street, walk up the path and ring heavily on Napoleon's bell. Nap said, "Oh, Christ. Her again," and sent Chris down, after a little thought, to get rid of her.

Chris sent the girl away and came back upstairs. He said, "Well, who was that?"

Nap lit himself another fag. "Aw, her name's Terry, I'm avoiding her. I owe her brother a bit of money, and I got drunk one night and told her I was in love with her. Like I said, I'm trying to avoid her. These things just happen to me, man. You know how I am."

They sat drinking more coffee for a while, and Nap said suddenly, "Christ, I'm fed up with drinking bloody coffee. I haven't had a proper drink in about two weeks. Why don't we go out to a pub or something? I'd rather get out of here for a while, anyway. I don't expect Terry really believed you. She'll probably be back later on."

"Christ, what're you running away from her for?"

"Oh, I dunno. I get fed up, I suppose. What I need's a girl who can take me for what I am and then leave me that way. All of them seem to wanna make great poets out of me, or great artists, or great writers. I don't know." He started laughing. "They all start off all right, just casual sex partners, then after a while they start wanting to move in with me permanently, or move me in with them. And then comes all the vows of faithfulness and the 'What were you doing walking around Trafalgar Square yesterday with that Indian girl with the long hair?' Man, it just smothers me."

"What you need's someone like Lorraine."

"Man, I thought that a long time ago."

They talked for a while and then left for a pub. Nap put on his own black, fur-lined parka. He looked at the parka Chris had just bought.

"You got a parka at last?" he said.

"Yeah, I just bought it."

They walked, chattering, through the streets. Chris said, "Why don't we get some drink and go back to our place? Spud's probably left some food behind—tins of soup or something. We can have something to eat, and I'll show ya that book."

"Yeah, all right, then."

They went into a tube station and then into a pub in Chelsea. They bought wine and some cider, and Chris said, "Let's have something to drink here, too. I'm feeling thirsty again."

"Get me a half of mild, then," Lorraine said.

Nap said, "Yeah, I'll have the same."

Chris bought the drinks, and they found somewhere to sit down. It was too early for the pub to be crowded. They sat by an empty fireplace, and Nap talked about the police and his ideas on anarchy. Napoleon was completely serious now. His anarchy was almost the most fervent thing in the whole of his life. Napoleon said,

"I've been thinking about joining the Y.C.L.—the Young Communist League. I always agreed with them before now on just about all their policies except for personal freedom. But now I'm not so sure. I've got an idea that what they believe in isn't so far from what I believe in after all. The Communists believe in anarchy just the same as I do. The only difference is that they believe in eventual anarchy through Communism.

"Someone was explaining it to me the other day— Ron, he's an artist. I'll introduce him to you someday. Anyway, he was trying to explain what he meant by Socialism to me. The way he explained it was like this: the ultimate aim of Socialism, or Communism if you want, is complete anarchy. But the Socialist argues that if a system of anarchy was to suddenly come into existence overnight, then it wouldn't be able to work because people wouldn't be ready for it. Therefore you have to have a transitional period of Communism first, to prepare people for the complete freedom of anarchy.

"Somehow I could never quite swallow any of this before, but now I'm not so sure. People always think they're so free in this country, but how free are they really? The way I see it, people aren't really much freer in Britain—or in America, for that matter—than they would be in Russia. At least if you thought your lack of freedom was getting you somewhere, if you thought that it was a way of gaining total freedom, as people in Russia think it is, then it might be worthwhile. Whereas in this country we just muddle along in the same old, semifree way with no definite end to it.

"After all, how free are we at the moment? How free do you feel?"

Chris said, "Yeah, I know what you mean. In this country there's a great appearance of freedom—everyone's made to think they're free—and yet when it comes down to it, you're probably just as likely to have false evidence planted on you by the British police as you are by the Russian or the Hungarian, or the Outer Mongolian, for that matter."

Chris sipped at his drink. Lorraine was lying back against the wall, her feet up on the base of another chair. Nap drank some of his beer and replaced his half-empty glass on the table.

Lorraine said to Chris, "You remember Jim, down in Stevenage? He was in a C.N.D. march once, him and a load of his friends. Some of them were picked up by the police. They didn't arrest them. They just wanted 'em for questioning. Then after they'd finished questioning them, they said they wanted to take their fingerprints. They didn't have any legal right to take the fingerprints, but they wanted them all the same. In the end they said if they didn't give permission to have their fingerprints taken, then they'd rip out their fingernails on one hand and say it just happened in a struggle."

Nap drank more of his beer. He said, "It's the sort of thing that happens all the time. But tell people these things, and they just don't believe you."

Chris nodded. They finished drinking and left for the flat, talking still about the police. On the way they realized that they were almost out of cigarettes and stopped off at another pub.

When they got to the flat, it was about eight o'clock. They passed around one of the wine bottles, and then Lorraine made black coffee while Chris opened a tin of soup. All of them were hungry, and they ate the soup out of a saucepan with three spoons.

"We ought to have bought some bread or something," Lorraine said.

"Yeah. It's too late now, though. We'll be leaving tomorrow, anyway. Be a waste of time getting anything then."

They flopped down in the kitchen and dining room. There was one armchair and two hard wooden chairs which folded up like deck chairs. Napoleon took the armchair, and Chris and Lorraine sat on the old carpet on the floor. They lit cigarettes and opened another bottle of wine.

Napoleon said, at about eleven o'clock, "I reckon it's about time I went home."

Lorraine said, "You don't wanna go all the way back to Putney. You might as well stay the night here."

"Yeah, stay the night here. I gotta go back tomorrow. You can come and see me off."

Napoleon settled himself back more comfortably in his chair. He said, "All right, then. What time tomorrow are ya going?"

"Sometime tomorrow morning, I s'pose. I'll have to phone up and find out about the trains. As long as I can get to Edinburgh sometime before Tuesday, it's all right."

Chris chain-smoked another three cigarettes as they sat there talking. About half past eleven, Lorraine decided to go to bed. She took a drink from the last remaining bottle of cider and then disappeared into the next room. Chris got up and walked to the window to draw the curtains. He stood for a moment, looking out at the streets. Napoleon watched him. Chris put on some records, and they sat in silence for a while.

Nap said, "Why'd you come down?"

"How d'you mean?"

"Well, it's a bloody long way to come, all the way down from Edinburgh."

"Yeah, I s'pose it is." Chris told him briefly about Carol and the party. He said, "I just seem to get these sudden urges to do things, like suddenly deciding that I wanted to hitchhike down to Stevenage. It wasn't so much that I had a sudden desire to come down to Stevenage again, or even to see Lorraine. It was more that

I just wanted to get out of Edinburgh suddenly. I wanted to be able to sit by the side of the A1, waiting for a lift, watching the passing traffic. Even if I hadn't got any farther than a couple of miles out of Edinburgh, then I would have been happy. Just sitting there by the side of the road, strumming on my guitar, watching the smoke rising up from the end of my fag."

"Sounds to me like you've been getting to feel too depressed."

"Yeah, exactly. I get these sudden feelings of great depression—usually brought on by something small and stupid, something which shouldn't depress me at all—and then to get rid of this depression I feel I have to do something, make some sort of sudden, ridiculous gesture to the world, to get me back to normality."

Napoleon said, "You serious about all this? You really worried about it? Or d'you think it's just something that's going to pass?"

"Oh"—Chris struggled for the words—"Oh, I don't know how to express it all. I don't think it's anything anyone else can help me with. I know the only person who can do anything about it is myself. And yet sometimes—I don't know—sometimes it gets to the sort of pitch where I think that perhaps I'm going mad. And when I do think this, when I try to think about it logically, it seems to me that perhaps going mad would be about the best thing that could happen to me. It would be a sort of escape, a sort of release. Perhaps madness is just my natural way out. And if so, why the hell am I fighting it? I look at myself sometimes, try to think of myself as if I was a completely different person, and I just come up with this one conclusion: If I didn't know better, then I'd say this person was at least partially insane. That's not so good, Nap. When you get to the stage of thinking like that about yourself—"

Nap didn't say anything, just waited for Chris to go on.

Chris said, "Tell me what you're thinking, Nap."

Nap looked across at the record player. The song had finished, and the record was just going around noiselessly, the odd scratching sound coming from the needle.

"I'm just glad I'm not you," Napoleon said. His voice was very quiet, very solemn. He handed the cider bottle over, and his voice changed. "Come on, have another drink."

"Yeah, why not?" Chris took the bottle and held the mouth of it tight against his lips. "What's wrong with being mad, anyway? I can still drink."

They turned off the record player and went in to see Lorraine. At ten o'clock the next morning they stood on King's Cross Station and checked up the time of Chris' train. They bought tea and something to eat in the buffet.

At ten forty-five Chris got into the train, and it began to pull out of the station. Lorraine walked back toward the buffet with Napoleon.

"I think he needs a holiday," Lorraine said.

"His way of life is a holiday. Take that away from him, and you'll just make things worse."

"You really think so?"

"Like he said to me last night, if you give him long enough, then one way or another he can work things out for himself."

VI

The next two weeks seemed to pass very quickly for Chris. They traveled and slept by day and worked by night. In Lanark and Kinross, Chris was pulled off the stage by girl fans. In Stirling, Chris and Dave walked into an all-night coffee bar after the show and got involved in a fight. In Glasgow the stage was invaded once again by girls, and Pete was pulled to the floor and his jacket ripped from his back. Each night they would spend in some hotel, and then the next morning they would drive on in the direction of the next town. Chris sat most of the time on the coach next to Dave or Pete, writing. By the end of the third week he'd finished the book and sent it back to Lorraine in Stevenage. Spud was back from New York, and he got a letter from the two of them.

Spud's having the book typed up for you. We're going up to London in a couple of days time and Spud reckons we should show the book to a publisher.

—Lorraine.

Chris read the letter on the coach. It had been sent to him at Lanark and then sent on from there to Stirling. By the time the end of the tour came, Chris was beginning to feel sad about it all. The atmosphere during the last two weeks was strange, stranger even than on the first part of the tour. Chris would stand on the stage for whole minutes sometimes, completely unaware of where he was or what he was meant to be doing. But the audience loved it all the same. One night he went onto the stage with a painful, nagging headache. He had had the headache all day. When he got onto the stage, he found the noise and the excitement almost too much for him. On his second show of that night he took on a chair and played sitting down, a bottle of wine on the floor by his side. When he had finished playing, he rushed off the stage as quickly as he could and headed for his dressing room. A reporter stopped him in the corridor and tried to ask polite questions about rumors that he was ill. Chris swore madly at him and told him to print whatever lies he wanted. When he got to his dressing room, he collapsed on the floor.

At Glasgow, at the end of the tour, Deene came up

to Chris to say his good-byes. Chris had grown to like Deene during the tour. They went into the bar at the hotel and bought drinks. There was a sort of general sadness about the end of the tour. Chris would have liked it to end in a great party running on and on for days. But Deene had to fly to London for a television show. Dave and Jim of the Representative had to record an interview for the pirate radio station Radio Scotland, and the others were making their plans for going home.

Chris sat in the hotel with Deene, and they talked about the tour.

"I've wanted to work with you for a long time," Deene said. "Glad I finally made it."

"Why don't you come and see us in London in about a week's time? We'll have a night out somewhere. Lorraine used to listen to your shows years ago on Luxembourg when you were over here in about 1962 or '63. She didn't realize till the last time I saw her that it was the same person. She's been wanting to meet you."

"I'd like to, but I have to get back to New York. My permit runs out in a couple of days' time, and there's a New York radio show lined up."

They drank their beer. Pete came in with Dave and sat with them for a while while Dave went to finish packing. Pete decided to go to Edinburgh with Chris before leaving for London. They talked about the time in Lanark when Chris had been dragged from the stage by the horde of excited fans. Deene had grabbed the microphone and tried to restore order. A girl near to the microphone had taken Deene by the legs and tried to drag him from the stage, too.

Pete laughed at the memory of it. When their drinks were finished, Pete bought more, and they sat and smoked. It was a Wednesday morning. The last show had been the night before, and everybody was preparing to leave. By the afternoon, only Chris, Pete and Deene were left. They said good-bye in the entrance to the hotel. Deene got into his taxi, and Pete and Chris reentered the hotel.

Their packing was already done. Pete said, "We can get a train to Edinburgh and get into a hotel for the night."

"What ya doing in London? You're not working again for a week or so, are ya?"

"We do an appearance at the Marquee Club on Saturday afternoon. It's only an appearance, though. We don't sing or anything. I don't s'pose Dave'll even turn up."

They got the train to Edinburgh and got into a hotel. Chris loved Edinburgh. He had liked the place ever since the first time he'd been there. As soon as they arrived he phoned Carol, and she arranged to meet him that night in the Hideaway on St. Andrew's Street.

Chris sat in the hotel with Pete.

"You taking her down to London with us?"

"She said she wanted to go down south somewhere. I don't know whether she'll be able to come, though. Her parents are terrible, as bad as Lorraine's. Sometimes I wish I could pick up rich birds or birds who could look after themselves a bit more, the way Nap does."

Pete grinned and said, "Yeah, I know what you mean. Nap seems to draw 'em to him just like a lump of bloody flypaper."

"Yeah. He still seems to spend his life running around in circles, trying to get away from 'em, though."

"Aw, Nap gets tired too easy. He was talking about going to Paris when I saw him about six weeks ago."

"He didn't say anything about it when I saw him in London."

"Like I said, he gets tired of things too easy. Probably he's changed his mind. He wanted to go to Paris and find some French hippie bird to sleep with under a bridge somewhere on the Left Bank of the Seine." Pete did an imitation of Nap's face when he was talking about sex.

"Aw, Nap's great," Chris said. "One day he'll be famous."

"Yeah, maybe one day we all will."

They left later on for the café on St. Andrew's Street. The place was a basement of two rooms, one of them containing a jukebox. Carol was already there, and Chris sat with her in a far corner of the larger room. She was quiet. They drank Coca-Cola for a while. Chris sat and looked at her.

"What you decided?" he said.

"I've had an argument with them at home. They know I was with you that night in the hotel. Kathy's Mum found out somehow, and she told my parents."

"Oh, Christ. What'd they say?"

"Nothing much. They think you're a bloody modern-day Rasputin, or something like that. They don't know anything about the baby yet. Me Dad told me the other day that if I was gonna go around with people like you, then I'd better pack me things and get out."

"You sure you're pregnant?"

"I haven't come on yet. Anyway, it doesn't matter. I wanna leave home, anyway. They won't care. They'll be glad to get rid of me. I won't tell 'em I'm going, I'll just go."

One of the records started to play. On her index finger Carol was wearing a large blue-colored ring. She saw him looking at it, and she took it off. The ring was too big even for her index finger. She put it on the table.

"What's that?"

"I got it from a boy I know." Carol smiled as she looked down at it. Chris felt happier to see her smiling.

She leaned forward, her elbows resting on the table. "He was Turkish," she said. "I knew him about a year ago."

Chris looked at the ring. It had the face of an Egyptian mummy. The face was blue, streaked with black, and around it there was a circular ring of white.

She said, "I can't wear it. It's too big. You might as well have it."

"Oh, Christ, no. You don't have to bribe me just to take you down to London."

She raised her eyes. "I'm not bribing you. I'd just like you to have it."

He slipped the ring onto his finger. "Why'd he give it to you in the first place? He must've wanted you to keep it."

"No, it wasn't like that. It was just that he always seemed to be wearing it. And it was so big that it seemed to get in the way. He used to scratch me every time he ran his fingers down me back." They grinned. "He was a student in London. He came here for the Edinburgh Festival. One afternoon I went out along the beach with him, near Cramond Island. There's some woods there, just past the pipeline. They belong to Lord someone-or-other's estate. Anyway, we went into the woods together. He was my first."

Chris was looking at the ring. He twisted it on his finger. He said, "It was almost the same as that for me."

"How d'you mean?"

"Oh, never mind. I'll tell you about it some other time." His mind was going back over the years, raking over the dead ashes of his memory. He remembered the first girl he'd fucked. It was years ago, so long that the details were almost all forgotten. All he could remember now were the myths and trappings of it. He said, "There weren't all that much to it, really. I reckon everyone's first time's more or less the same. I s'pose it could have been the twenty-first time, really. It didn't mean anything."

He looked down at his packet of Player's No. 6 and took one out.

He offered her one, and they smoked.

"When are you going?" Chris said.

"I'm not sure. I want a couple of days to get ready."

Chris said, "I was gonna go back tomorrow with Pete. You'll be able to get down all right by yourself, won't ya?"

"Yeah, of course I will. I'll come by train. You haven't given me the address, though."

He wrote out the address for her. "You got enough money for the train fare?"

"Sure, I'll be all right."

"You're sure?"

"Yeah, of course." She looked resolved, decided. Chris hoped things would work out all right for her. He looked across into her eyes. He thought that perhaps she was just a little bit in love with him. She was.

147

In a way, just about every girl who came to his concerts was a little bit in love with him. The realization made him feel strange, unnatural. Him, Pete, Dave, all the others, in a way they were all purveyors of a sort of sex or love. Chris looked down at the ring and then over toward the counter where the coffee and the Coca-Colas were.

"You want another drink?"

"Yeah. I'll buy 'em this time." She went over and bought the drinks. He watched her come back and sit down. In the other room he could see Pete, standing against the wall, talking to a pair of girls. Suddenly he realized how similar Pete was to himself. Pete was going through a period of depression and frustration, too. He thought back to that night when they'd sat together in his dressing room, talking about nirvana. Then he thought about the days when they'd first met, when Pete had been the great up-and-coming pop star, pop spokesman to the world, and Chris had been a hated, loved figured just recently acquitted of murder for lack of evidence. He remembered the hours they'd spent with Lorraine and Spud, sitting in coffee bars, musing about life and death, about folk music and the world in general. He wondered if Pete could see it all coming in the way that he could, the time when they would be old men, pointed out on the streets sometimes: "They were both famous men once. I remember them coming to Edinburgh together on one of the old one-night tours.

I was about six years old then. Of course they don't do any work now. They went out long ago, about the same time as the Beatles."

Chris started on his drink. Carol sat opposite him again. Her eyes were green. It was the first time that he'd noticed them. He ran his eyes over the whole of her body, all that he could see of her above the table. Pete came over to them eventually and sat himself down. The girls he'd been chattering to stayed where they were, chattering to each other in the smaller room.

"Let's go to a pub," Pete said. "I feel like getting myself drunk tonight."

"You bringing them two birds with ya?"

"Aw, not tonight. I don't feel in the mood. They make me feel like some strange new type of kangaroo or something on show in a zoo."

Carol said, "I know a pub we can go to. It's not all that far. Come on, I'll show you."

They left the café and got out into the street again. Chris put his parka on and walked along with the loose green cloak blowing out behind him in the wind. The nights were beginning to get colder. Pete lit himself a cigarette as he was walking and warmed his hands around the flickering match.

They got to the pub, and Chris said, "What d'you want to drink?"

"Get me whiskey will ya, Chris?"

Chris bought Pete's whiskey and got two ciders for

himself and Carol. Coming back to their table, Chris realized that Pete was almost asleep. The drink seemed to revive him for a while, and then he sat back sleepily again. Chris began to feel sleepy himself. In his pocket he had some pills. He took them out and let Pete see them.

Pete said, "Yeah, I could do with some."

It was too crowded to take them in the bar. They went into the toilet and swallowed some of the pills. When they came out, Pete bought another round of drinks. He said to Chris, "Have whiskey this time."

"No, I don't want whiskey. Brown ale."

They sat at the table and drank their second drinks. They drank quickly, and all of them were quiet. After a while Chris began to feel drunk. There was no excitement or ecstasy in it for him, but it made everything seem less painful to him. The drink clouded his mind and prevented him from thinking. When he wanted to see the time from the clock up on the wall, he found it hard to concentrate. It was difficult for his eyes to focus properly, and he had to force himself into concentration. The time was ten o'clock. They had been drinking for forty minutes. He couldn't remember how many drinks they'd had. Pete was now drinking beer again. His face had an expression of blankness, complete calm. The pills were beginning to work. Chris could feel them working on himself, too.

Carol hadn't drunk as much as the other two. She was more in control of herself, almost unaware of how drunk Pete and Chris were. Chris gulped down the drink in front of him and made to stand up. He said, "Come on, we oughta be getting back. Buy some wine, and we'll take it with us."

Pete said, "Yeah, sure." He staggered to his feet, picked up his glass and finished off his drink.

They bought some wine and got out into the street. Out in the street, Chris made an effort to clear his mind. The cold air helped him, and soon the feeling of drunkenness seemed to pass. He looked over at Pete, but Pete seemed to be as high as ever. If they'd wanted they could have caught a bus, but Chris preferred to walk. Carol walked part of the way with them until they got to the corner where she had to turn off.

Chris said to her again, "You're sure you'll be all right?"

"Yeah, I'll be all right. Go home. You're drunk."

He said good-bye to her, and she disappeared into a bus line. Chris and Pete walked on. They got to the hotel again, and being inside seemed to make Pete feel worse. They went upstairs. Their two rooms had a connecting door, and they sat in Chris' room and tried to open the wine. Pete flopped down into a chair. He looked suddenly exhausted. Chris sat down, too. He opened one of the wine bottles, took a gulp of the wine and handed it over to Pete.

151

Pete didn't take the bottle straightaway. He said, "What d'you think of suicide, Chris?"

"What d'you mean?"

Pete took the wine. He said, "I stole something out of a book shop once. I was seven years old. I did it about four times. On the fourth time I got caught by the manager of the shop. He called the police. A policewoman came along. She took my name and everything, sent me home, and said the police would be coming around to see my parents later that night. When I got home, the disgrace just seemed too much. I decided I was going to kill myself. I wasn't any good at it. I remembered those warnings they used to have on plastic bags about keeping them away from young children in case they put them over their heads. I tried to put a plastic bag over my head, but it wasn't any good. At the last moment I always pulled the bag off my head. After that I tried to electrocute myself. It sounds stupid. But that didn't work either. I got a shock which just picked me up and tossed me over onto the other side of the room. But after that I was too scared of electricity to ever try it again. I still wanted to kill myself, but I couldn't bring myself to face the electric shock." Pete's hair had fallen down across his ears. He looked very wild, very tired, suddenly.

"I remember I just sat there on the side of my bed. Probably I cried. I wanted to kill myself still. I wanted to die, just vanish. And yet I felt tired, just like I do

152

now. All the attempts I'd made had left me feeling desperate and exhausted. And something made me remember all that tonight. I don't know what it was. I always remember things like that when I'm drunk. But what I'm trying to say is this: Sometime tonight—when I was standing talking to those girls, I think—I just got this sudden feeling of complete sickness and nausea. And I felt exactly the same as I did twelve years ago. I felt that the only thing left for me to do with my life was end it. I think I felt the same way as you were telling me you felt when you were standing on the rocks on Cramond Island the night of the party. I looked at myself in complete detachment. I didn't have any feelings either way on whether I lived or died. And it suddenly came to me that if everyone had the courage to look at life this way all the time instead of just in odd, sudden flashes, then the whole population of the world would commit suicide tomorrow."

He suddenly realized that he had the wine bottle still in his hand. He took a gulp of the wine and handed it to Chris.

Pete said, "Quite seriously, I think I'm nearer to suicide tonight than I have been ever since that time when I was seven years old. I felt tonight for the first time that time was really against me. In about five months' time I'll be twenty years old. So will you. Dave will be twenty-one. Jim'll be about the same age as me and you. How much longer d'you think people are gonna buy our records? Gradually we're gonna slip, further and further. The one-night stands are gonna get less and less. All the birds standing around waiting to go to bed with us are gonna get fewer and fewer. Until in the end there's gonna be just nothing left. I can see it happening already. It hasn't happened to you yet. They still see you as being their hero, their spokesman. You're still the rebel with the long hair, the poet with the guitar. But the Representative are just another group like all the rest. We're better than some. I know that. Once we were heralded as the best group in the country. We were top of the polls for two years. This year probably we'll be second. Next year, fifth. The year after that—nothing. All the good things are behind us. It's all farcical. It's like the fall of the Ottoman Empire, the Sick Man of Europe, the sacking of Rome. Nothing seems to be the same anymore. I can see us doing another tour like this one in about a year's time. All the faces will just be boredom. And probably my face will get as bored as the audience's. I can't take that, Chris. How can you resign yourself to being old and useless at the age of twenty?" He leaned forward and put his hands up to his forehead.

Chris didn't know what to say. The wine had acted quickly, and both of them were drunk again. Chris had a headache. Pete had one, too. Chris finished the first bottle of wine and dropped it on the floor. He picked up the other bottle and opened it. The cork came out with a pop, and the wine spilled over their legs.

Chris said, "Man, what you're looking for is paradise, and if we committed suicide, then paradise ain't where we'd go to."

"Aw, talk sense, man, I'm serious."

"Well, what can we do? I feel exactly the same way as you do. There ain't nothing we can do about it. I got theories and ideas, but what are they? Just theories. If you're Spud, you can smoke hash and find paradise that way. If you're Ramakrishna, you can go into a temple outside Calcutta. If you're Buddha, you can sit under some sacred tree. But we're Pete Stewart and Chris Plater. What the hell can we do about it all? All the world can do for us is to say, 'Believe in Christ,' or 'Meditate before the Buddha,' or 'Go into a monastery.' None of that does any good to us at all. You can't find your nirvana by trying to copy the way Buddha found his. And if you don't manage to find your own kind of nirvana, then you'll never be able to get rid of your frustrations and periods of depression. But it's all just a load of talk. Everyone knows all that, anyway. We might just as well shoot ourselves now."

Chris took a gulp of the wine. He yawned and handed it over to Pete. Pete took the wine and drank some of it. Chris' eyes could hardly keep open. He looked at Pete through his half-closed eyes. Pete looked tired, depressed, unhappy. He put his hand up to his head again. Chris took out some cigarettes and lit one for Pete.

"Thanks, Chris."

They sat there in silence. Finally Pete said, "Oh, I'm going to bed." He got up and steadied himself. He took a last drink of the wine and staggered toward the door. He touched Chris on the shoulder as he passed.

"See ya in the morning, Pete."

"Yeah, see ya, Chris."

Chris drained the last of the wine and collapsed on his bed. When he woke up, it was late the next morning. He looked around him to try to judge the time. A sharp pain shot through his head. He forced himself off the bed and got himself a drink of water. When he'd finished drinking, he pushed open the connecting door and went into Pete's room.

Pete was asleep on the floor. Chris sat on the bed to ease the pain in his forehead. An empty aspirin bottle lay at Pete's side. Chris ran his hand again over his head. Suddenly realization dawned over him. He looked back at the empty bottle of pills. Pete was dead.

4. / *And Fall*

SWARMS and flurries of pigeons flew in the air over London's Trafalgar Square. On the side of the square nearest to the National Gallery, the hippie girls in their torn blue jeans and their bare feet stood with their males, arguing in groups, or sat on the seats, sleeping. The foreign tourists took their pictures of London from a distance, sitting on a step or leaning against a wall. The hippies smoked stolen fags and talked among themselves, ignoring everything.

Chris envied them. He lurched against the bowl of one of the two fountains. Eventually he sat himself on the edge of the fountain and buried his head in his hands. He was drunk. He'd been drinking all the dinner hour—and all the night before.

He looked up at the people around him. One of the hippie girls was looking at him, probably because of the guitar resting against the fountain between his feet. He lowered his eyes and gazed down at the ground. A pair of girls with sleeping bags walked past him in a sort of circle around the fountain. Policemen watched from every corner of the square, mingling with the crowds yet remaining aloof and watchful. The pigeons landed, scurried, and took off again in droves. Chris looked up. One of the policemen approached the two girls with the sleeping bags. Chris could imagine what was going on. The girls looked about sixteen or seventeen years old.

"All right, you two, how old are you?"

"Eighteen."

"Oh, yes. Can you prove it?"

"What d'we have to prove it for?"

"You've left home, have you?"

"Yeah."

"Where d'you come from?"

"Watford."

"So you thought you'd leave home and go on the road, did ya? Come on then, let's see some proof you're over seventeen. National Insurance cards, birth certificates, passports."

The girls and the policeman stood arguing in the middle of the square. The policeman pointed several times to their sleeping bags and to the duffel bag that one of the girls was carrying. Another policeman approached them, and all four walked off to the police box at the corner of the square, the girls walking reluctantly between the two men.

Chris lit another cigarette. Expressionless, he watched the parade of people in their gaily colored Carnaby street clothes passing through Trafalgar Square. Robby Truman, a poet from Cornwall who slept on benches in Waterloo Station and lived on the food he stole out of supermarkets, stood over by one of the drinking fountains, talking to another poet, Robert Mills, who believed in God. Chris had met them both in some other world. One of Spud's girl friends had loaned her typewriter to Robby Truman, and he'd spent a whole weekend typing up his poems on her bedroom floor. Chris looked over again at the hippie girls on the benches by the steps coming down from the road.

He felt sick. Pete was dead. The sentence repeated itself in his mind. It was almost two weeks now. Or was it longer? The days passed by him almost as if he were in a dream. He remembered when he'd gotten to London and seen Carol. She'd read about it in the newspapers before she'd left Edinburgh. She was staying now at the flat. The first day they had been in the flat together, he'd hardly even known that she was there. Lorraine was in Stevenage still with her parents. He'd written to her, and she'd written back to say she'd be coming down to London again as soon as she could get away. That was two weeks ago. Since then he'd just drifted around London, hardly speaking to anyone. Spud had come back from America and brought back a picture of himself done by a girl in Greenwich Village. He'd read about Pete in the papers. Chris focused his eyes on the cigarette hanging from his mouth. Why was everything so unreal? Why did everything seem so superficial to him suddenly? He felt that he was just a puppet figure being manipulated in the throes of someone else's dream. The death of Pete had made him feel that his words—his words, Pete's words, Spud's words—all of them were more than just words suddenly. They had caused Pete's suicide. Pete had resolved all their fine words into death. It came to Chris suddenly that the time when he could just talk was over. What was the point of it all? He looked up at the sky, at the swarm of pigeons flying overhead. He felt a sense of the great openness of everything, the total vastness of life, of his own mind.

He threw away his cigarette end and immediately lit himself another cigarette. The hippie girl who'd been watching him said something to a boy next to her and began to walk over toward him.

"Can ya lend us sixpence, mate? We're trying to get enough for three cups of coffee."

"Yeah, sure." Chris pulled his loose change from out of his pocket. He had a few pennies, a two-shilling piece and a six-penny bit. "Here y'are. I don't need it. You might as well have it all."

She said, "We only need sixpence. We've got the rest of the money." Her voice was sweet, like Lorraine's.

Chris said, "It's all right. I won't need it. I been on the road meself. You won't get much with two bob, but you might as well take it."

He handed her the money, and she said, "Thanks," and took it.

She said, "I'll buy a couple of tins of soup. We ain't had anything to eat in two days." She looked at him. She said, "You're Chris Plater, ain't you?"

"Yeah."

She nodded to the guitar. "Could ya play us something?" She sat against the bowl of the fountain as she said it, lighting herself a cigarette. Her sandaled feet brushed the edge of Chris' jeans.

"Aw, it's too crowded," Chris said. He didn't want to play anything at the moment. He didn't feel in the mood.

"Come over there and play," she said. She pointed to the collection of hippies where she'd been standing before.

"I don't feel in the right sort of mood at the moment. I feel a bit depressed."

"Because of Pete Stewart?"

"Yeah." He didn't ask her how she knew about Pete. Everyone knew about it, anyway. She would have read about it in the papers.

"Come over, anyway," she said.

Chris was glad she didn't say anything more about Pete, didn't ask him how it happened or whether he'd been there at the time. He said, "Yeah, all right."

They walked over to the others. The girl introduced them all very briefly. "I'm Jill. This is Smudge . . . Don."

The other two had been arguing about the birth pill. Smudge was small, dark-haired and very pale. Don was clean-shaven and wore old corduroy trousers, frayed and dirty. He offered Chris his hand, and they stood there, shaking hands profoundly.

Jill said, "Let's get that coffee."

"Yeah."

The moved off and walked toward Piccadilly. Chris allowed himself to be swept along with the crowd. He felt like a piece of wood thrown into a river and being carried along by the current, like a dead body being swept along with the tide, being washed up onto the beach. Jill walked next to him. She said, "We've got a flat in Fulham. The rent's paid for two more months. Then we have to get out."

He carried his guitar between their two bodies. The thing banged against Jill's legs as they walked. She said, "Christ, carry that thing on the other side." He did. They crossed Piccadilly and into Soho. It was about four in the afternoon, and the streets were crowded. It seemed as if the whole population of Soho must be made up of tourists.

Chris said, "Fucking tourists. Why don't they go to the London Zoo or something?"

"They like to come and see how the immoral Londoners live. The swinging city. What a load of fucking rubbish."

Don and Smudge disappeared somehow in the crowd ahead. Don's long, fair hair bobbed out for a minute from behind a police helmet, and then it was lost again. Someone bumped into Chris and stopped him.

"D'you think I could have your autograph?"

"Er—yeah, sure." Chris gave the girl his autograph. She seemed to have the idea that he was Bob Dylan's cousin. Jill waited for him while he signed his name. The girl thanked him. He said, " 'S all right," and then they walked on.

"You're a painter?" he said to Jill suddenly.

"Yeah. How did you know?"

"Just guessed. What d'ya paint?"

They walked on along the streets. "Oh, people," Jill said. "I did a picture of Don. Sold it for ten guineas." She talked on about her paintings. Chris walked beside her in silence. He found it was an effort to listen to what she was saying. His mind wandered from incident to incident, over the happenings of the last few months.

They got to a café and Smudge and Don were already inside. Jill bought the coffees, and they sat talking. Chris' feeling of morbidness seemed to affect them all. Don and Smudge were leaving later in the afternoon for Southend. They were going by tube to Tottenham and getting a lift from there. Chris found himself talking with Don about death. At the end of it he felt sickened by the pointlessness of it all. Words, words, words. What was the use of them all? They changed the conversation back to Jill's paintings. In the end Don and Smudge had to leave to get to Tottenham. Chris sat in the café with Jill.

She said, "Will you come back to Fulham with me and have a look at some of the paintings?"

"I ought to get home. I don't wanna be wandering around London later on tonight. I'm feeling tired."

She shrugged her shoulders. She said, with no expression in her voice, "If you want, you could spend the night in Fulham." He looked at her, and he saw that the expression which should have been in her voice was in her eyes.

"Yeah, all right," he said. He smiled at her weakly. For some reason he wanted to say, "Thanks," on the end of the sentence. But she would have just laughed at him and said, "Thanks for what?"

They left Soho and got on a tube. They had given the rest of the money to Smudge and Don to get them to Tottenham. Chris said, "There won't be anyone at the other end wanting to see our tickets, will there?"

"There might be. It's the rush hour. Doesn't matter, though. We'll get through with the crowds."

A train came in, and they got inside with the crowds. They stood up by the doors until Earl's Court, and then they changed trains.

Chris sat with his guitar on his lap, sheltering it from the pressing rush-hour crowds. He read the adverts as they came into each new station. The reflection of Jill stared at his own reflection in the window opposite. They reached Fulham and pushed past the ticket collector amidst the horde of shoppers and college students and City businessmen. Outside it looked as if it were about to rain. They walked quickly toward Jill's flat.

She unlocked the door and let him in. The room was large, with a double bed on one side by the drawn curtains and odd paintings and portraits propped up against the walls. Off to one side of the room there was an open doorway leading to another, smaller room with a single bed. Jill lit a fag and offered him one.

"Thanks."

"D'you want coffee? There's no milk, but I can make it black."

"I'll make it if you like." He dropped his guitar on the bed and went over with her to the gas ring. Chris put on the kettle of water, and Jill got out the coffee.

"Reach up for that cheese, will ya?"

He got down the cheese and a half-eaten loaf of bread. Jill made the coffee, and Chris cut off two hunks of the bread and two hunks of cheese. They sat on the bed and ate their bread and cheese. Chris looked at the pictures scattered around the room. He got up and walked over to the paintings on the opposite side of the room. Jill followed him. She knocked ash from the end of her cigarette onto the floor. Chris stood there, his two thumbs tucked into the belt loops of his jeans.

"What d'ya think?" she said.

"I think you oughta meet a friend of mine—Spud. He's just come back from New York. He used to do some paintings himself, about six months ago. Why don't you try and get an exhibition?"

"I've had one. Sold a few abstract things, but I've given up doing them now. I'd rather just do straight-forward portraits, but people just don't seem to be interested in them anymore."

He walked around the room, looking at the rest of the paintings. Jill sat back on the bed. She picked up his guitar.

"Play something for us."

He went back and took the guitar from her. She watched him as he toyed around with it, strumming at the strings.

"What d'you want me to play?"

"Anything."

Softly, he began to play the introduction to a song.

It was "She Belongs to Me." He smiled as he began to sing. The words came easily to him, effortlessly. He paused for a moment, his eyes far off in the distance as he strummed on the guitar.

Suddenly he put down the guitar and turned away from her. He said, "Oh, I forget the words. I don't wanna do any more." He sat down next to her on the bed. "Sorry. I dunno, I just don't feel in the right sort of mood. All I wanna do tonight is just get in some girl's fucking bed and—" He caught her eye. "Oh, never mind. I'm just feeling morbid. Let's have another fag."

They lit two more cigarettes.

Jill said, "Why did Pete Stewart kill himself?"

"He was feeling depressed. We both were. We'd been out drinking, and then we brought home a bottle of wine and got even more drunk than ever. We were talking about pop groups and life and the purpose behind everything, and Pete was talking about suicide and—" He shrugged his shoulders. "I went into his room the next morning, and he was dead."

Neither of them spoke. The coffee was cold, and Jill made some more. When she sat down, she said, "I think I know how you feel."

"How d'you mean?"

"I think you were probably thinking about suicide yourself that night. I saw you during that tour you did of Scotland. I hitched up to Dundee with another girl just to see you. You looked on the stage as if—I don't know. As if you felt just the way that it sounded as if Pete felt when you were talking about him just now.

"You looked as if you were a million miles away. When you sang 'Mr. Tambourine Man,' you sounded almost as if you actually believed that Mr. Tambourine Man existed. I read a poem of yours once—'The Golden Realm of Dreams'—where you prayed to be transported away somewhere into the realm of dreams. 'I pray for sleep to save my body from this hick-land dome of reasoning/Transport me to the hilltop in the golden realm of dreams.' It seemed as if that was what you were feeling then. You were looking for some form of release, some way of saving yourself from the depression you were feeling. You looked as if you were probably drugged, and yet through the drugs you could see yourself exactly as you were, perhaps see yourself clearer than if you'd been sober. And you seemed to realize that you couldn't go on feeling the way you were. It's difficult to say what I mean, but I think you were unhappy and depressed, and I think you probably realized that if you carried on feeling this way, then you'd probably end up committing suicide, too."

Chris took the coffee from her. He wanted her to go on talking. He didn't want to have to talk himself. He didn't feel capable of explaining it, didn't feel capable of working anything out, analyzing things, and yet he wanted to think about it, hear what she thought.

The fact that she'd asked him about Pete didn't seem to matter now. Chris remembered Pete lying there that morning, the bottle of pills next to him. He hid his face. The taste of the coffee in his mouth seemed antiseptic —cold, glowingly cold, like menthol cigarettes. He was talking suddenly, but for a moment he hardly even realized it was his own voice.

He said, "Pete seemed to be feeling . . . frustrated. All through the tour we were sharing rooms or fags together. Toward the end he got as depressed as me, perhaps worse. I don't know whether he felt the same, but I used to get periods of great excitement, great elation, and then immediately afterward there would be a period of great depression. It was like having sex. For a few moments everything was marvelous, and then afterward you just felt terrible. As if there was nothing you could do, nothing at all except die."

Chris drank some more of his coffee. He thought to himself, oh, fuck. What good does it do talking about it? He lit himself another cigarette. He handed it to Jill, and she took a single puff from it, running her finger over his hand as she handed it back to him.

She said, "How near are you to committing suicide yourself?" Her voice was very low, very serious.

Chris closed his eyes against the rising wall of cigarette smoke. He could feel a sort of nausea, or tired-ness, or perhaps just sickness at the word *suicide* sweep-ing over him.

"Don't talk about it," he said. "It's too heavy, too wordy, too—"

He couldn't finish the sentence. When they went to bed that night, they fucked and went to sleep almost instantly. About four o'clock Chris woke up. He lay there, thinking. He wanted a cigarette, but the packet was on the other side of the bed, and he couldn't reach it. He looked down at Jill. She had been marvelous. He felt disgusted with himself for sleeping with her. What was he? Some kind of monster who contaminated ev-eryone he came into contact with? Jill woke up, and they made love again, and then they got up and ate more cheese and went back to sleep. At nine o'clock the next morning he woke up again. Jill was asleep. Chris' eyes were bleared and strange. A feeling of utter repulsion came over him, repulsion for himself and for all his words and for all his actions. He got out of bed while she was still asleep and got dressed. He wanted to leave her a note or something. He found himself wanting to say thank you to her again. He started to look for something to write to her on. When he found something, he just stood for a moment, looking at it. He searched for a pen, and then he suddenly stopped, stood still for a minute and ran his hand, pressed tight against the skin of his scalp, back through his hair.

170

Jill groaned a couple of times and turned over in her sleep. He picked up his guitar, threw away the piece of paper and walked to the door.

II

For the next few days Chris wandered aimlessly. He woke up late every morning and sat with Carol, drinking coffee or eating in the flat. Then from about one o'clock he'd go out, walking around London, or sit indoors while Carol went out to see Spud, staring up at the ceiling and drinking more coffee. The painter, Jill, and the other two, Smudge and Don, slowly faded from his mind.

During the next week Lorraine came down. Chris went to news theaters with her on a couple of afternoons, just to pass the time, but after that he practically ignored her. There were a series of letters delivered at the flat for Spud from a man named Hoffner, but when Spud talked about them, Chris hardly even heard what he was saying.

He seemed to exist only in the shadowy world of his own imagination. Things passed by over his head. On one afternoon Carol had gone looking for a job and Spud and Lorraine were in Putney, looking for Napoleon. Chris sat on the bed, staring at the wall. He turned on the record player and put on some records. The day was cold and miserable. It was the end of the

English summer. The miserable, drab, overcast day seemed to reflect exactly the way Chris was feeling. He stared at the faded, torn wallpaper. Pete had committed suicide because he'd got nothing left to live for. What had Chris got to live for? Anything? He shook his head, as if there were actually another person in the room with him, asking him the question.

He thought back to a few days ago, when he'd had to go to some photographer to have pictures taken for his new L.P. and for the cover of his book. Sitting there as the pictures were being taken, he'd tried to remember exactly why the book and the songs on the record had been written. Had the meanings the songs held for him been so fleeting that he couldn't even remember what they were? He'd found himself sitting there, looking at the camera, smoking and thinking about it absently, his mind blank.

He was nineteen years old. What was he doing? Losing his memory already?

Chris sat on the bed. He leaned forward to the half-empty bottle of wine by the record player and pulled it over to him. He wanted to get drunk and then collapse in a sleeping heap on the bed—until the next morning, when he would wake up and get drunk again. "Why not?" he said out loud, looking at the wine. On the other side of the room there was a second bottle. He had bought them both the night before, for a party. But when he'd gotten home, he hadn't felt like a party anymore. He had just sat on the bed all evening, silent.

Chris took a first drink of the wine. He looked at the record player again, and then down at himself. He was wearing no socks, just a pair of sandals. The nails on his toes were long and needed cutting. He pulled out his shirt from his jeans and undid the buttons so that the shirt flopped down on either side of his body, against his hips. He looked down at his chest, at the small, semi-visible hairs growing down on his stomach, close against his skin. He pressed the wine bottle against his lips and tilted back his head.

He talked to himself.

"Dreams. Nightmares. Sometimes I think I'm going mad. . . . Sometimes I think I'd just like to be fucking mad. . . . Half the time I'm just acting to myself, acting out madness."

He faced the wall. He sat there with his hands against his head, the words coming out of him expressionlessly, long intervals between the sentences.

"Perhaps someone who wants to be mad—pretends to be mad—really is mad. Perhaps someone who sits drinking wine and talking to himself and wondering whether or not he's mad must have just been bloody insane at birth." He bowed his head over the bottle. "Oh, fuck it. It doesn't matter. There's no such thing as sanity. Some people are just more insane than others. How can anyone put up a dividing line and say, 'This side of the line it's sanity, that side it's madness'?"

He stood up. The bottle was empty now, and he tossed it back onto the bed. He opened the door and went out along the passage to the toilet.

As he was about to leave, he glimpsed suddenly his own reflection in the mirror on the bathroom door. He stood for a moment, looking at himself.

He said slowly, "They're saying you're ill, boy. Ill. That's the nice way they have of putting it. The music papers have got wind of it already. Soon there'll be a nice, gossipy article about it in the *Daily Mirror* with a picture of you to go with it—a picture of you with Lorraine probably, both of you standing with the wind in your faces, holding cigarettes. And underneath it they'll write CHRIS PLATER IN HAPPIER TIMES, WITH GIRL FRIEND LORRAINE BISHOP. . . . And what'll happen after that? There'll be silence for a few months, probably. And then perhaps they'll consider you're worth scribbling off another couple of columns about—all depending on how the fans react when they realize you can't write any decent songs anymore, and whether or not they walk out on you when you do one of your infrequent concert performances and they realize that you're blind drunk and your act is hardly worth listening to, anyway." He ran his hand down across his chest. He said, "Aw, make the sign of the cross, man, and die like Rasputin."

He went out into the hall and back to his room. The records were still playing. They had almost finished.

He took them off and put on an L.P. He got the other bottle and sat down again on the bed. He rolled over toward the bookcase and found himself a pen and a scrap of paper.

Dear Lorraine. I am going to kill myself. If anyone had told me that I was going to write those six words a couple of years ago, then I would have laughed in his face. If anyone had told me a few weeks ago that Pete Stewart was going to take an overdose of aspirins, then I would have called him a fool. But people change. Two years ago I was happy to wander the country as some sort of English gypsy, stealing, drinking and smoking. If it hadn't been for the policeman on Clacton beach, then perhaps I would have stayed like that. But I didn't. Perhaps that's his revenge.

My mind has been catching up on me, Lorraine. You know that because you've seen it happening. For the first time in my life, living has become painful to me. So I'm going to stop living. I'm going to do it the easy way, with aspirins. I want you to try and contact my cousin and tell him what's happened. Probably he'll be down in Folkestone.

Chris took a drink of the wine.

When I started writing this note, I suppose I wanted to write some sort of famous last letter. But letters are to be remembered by, and I think I'd rather be forgotten. I know that once I used to believe that there was some great purpose in life. I suppose I still do believe that. The only difference is that before I thought I was capable of discovering that purpose, and now I feel that I've gone as far in looking for that purpose as

I'm capable of going. Some gigantic barrier is being held up before me. Thus far and no farther. So for that reason I intend to commit suicide.

If, right now as I sit on the bed listening to "Tambourine Man" and feeling the way I used to feel before —that what Dylan is saying in this song is exactly what I've been meaning when I talk about finding a paradise and looking for my purpose—if, as I sit here, I happen to feel all this so strongly again that I decide to just tear up this letter and not commit suicide after all, then I know that within a couple of days, within a couple of months, I shall suddenly feel again exactly as I do now. Either that or the miracle will happen, and I will be able to recognize my paradise after all.

The whole thing is a question of strength, and I feel now that my strength has taken me as far as it is capable of taking me. Thus far and no farther. I thought I would be able to carry on until the end of the tunnel. But now I realize that I can't. These are all fucking words, and like all words they mean nothing. I love you, Lorraine. Goodbye.

He got up and looked at the piece of paper he held in his hand. "Mr. Tambourine Man" was finished. The L.P. was now playing another track. Chris turned off the record player and stood for a moment in silence.

He walked over to the chest of drawers by the window. He looked at himself in the mirror. The corners of his eyes were damp with tears. He opened the drawer and took out the aspirins. The almost full bottle stared up at him from the palm of his hand. He looked at himself again in the mirror. A feeling of desperation surged through him. He couldn't do it.

He opened the bottle and tipped out some of the aspirins into his hand. He couldn't do it; he knew he couldn't. He dropped everything into the drawer again and closed it quickly, his fingers gripped tight still around the handle of the drawer, holding it shut.

He picked up the letter from off the bed and screwed it up in his hand. He picked up his matches, threw the letter into the open fireplace and set a light to it.

Chris collapsed on the bed. He held his hands over his eyes. It was impossible. He couldn't go forward, he couldn't go backward, and he couldn't escape.

Chris shook off his clothes and climbed into the unmade bed. Crying, he eventually fell asleep, his letter ashes in the grate.

When Lorraine and Spud came in, it was a few hours later. Chris was still asleep. Spud went over to make coffee. Lorraine walked around to the other side of the bed to see if Chris was sleeping.

"He's in bed early, ain't he?"

Lorraine sat on the end of the bed. "Spud, you think he ought to go to a doctor?"

"He wouldn't go to one even if you told him to."

"He's ill, though."

They looked at each other. Deep down they were

both worried. Spud's face was tanned, almost red, the result of going to America. He brushed aside his long hair. He said, "You can't do anything, and neither can I. He works things out for himself. All you can do is leave him alone to get on with it."

"But what about the tours? You canceled with Hoffner, and now he's gonna sue. If Chris's got any more work to do this month, then he'll have to cancel out of that, too."

Spud looked over almost automatically to the boiling kettle. He said, "There's a couple of things I'll have to see to, not much. He's got a recording session sometime next week. I've postponed it." He looked over to Chris, lying asleep in the bed. "He can't work while he's feeling like this. All he wants is to be left alone so that he can work things out. Let him do it for himself, Lorraine. We can't help him with it."

III

Chris caught the tube from south Kensington to Piccadilly. It was morning, about ten o'clock. When he'd woken up, Lorraine had been asleep. Spud had been writing, and Carol had been out. He'd not seen Carol in something like two days. He had borrowed some cigarettes from Spud, and then he'd gone out.

From Piccadilly he crossed to Soho and found a

café. He bought Coke and sat smoking. The café was crowded. The walls were covered with pictures of old pop stars, a parade of lesser Elvis Presleys: Marty Wilde, Adam Faith, Cliff Richard, the idols of the late 1950's, when Chris had been still a kid in school. He looked over at an old advert on one of the walls: "Coming next week, Marty Wilde, the King of Rock." The poster was dated May 13, 1958. There was something nostalgic and yet impressive about the way the posters were still hanging there, like the statue of Nelson standing high still over Trafalgar Square, over a hundred and fifty years after the man had died.

Chris thought absently about the great Teddy Boy generation which had preceded his own. The gang fights had been just the same then, the roaring motor-bikes, the girls with their beehive hairdos, the tight jeans and leather jackets, the slashed cinema seats and the flick knives dipped in blood. Each generation thought that it was the first of its kind. Anti-Suez demonstrations gave way to nuclear disarmament and C.N.D. C.N.D. gave way to the war in Vietnam and the heyday of the anarchists and the Y.C.L.

Nothing changed. One day people would probably sit just where he was sitting now and say, "Of course I remember the good old 1960's. There was a kid called Chris Plater. They say he went mad in the end. He's probably sweeping the streets by now, of course. He used to always say he wasn't a singer, but a poet. I saw a concert of his once. He stood up on the stage, just smoking a cigarette and drinking water."

Chris drank some of his Coke. He thought back to the weekend in Brighton with Spud and Lorraine, the night he spent with Lorraine, sleeping under the tractor.

One of his own records came onto the jukebox. It was "Cry for a Shadow." He sat listening to it. Was it possible that that was really his voice? Were things really as simple as he made them seem on that record? He closed his eyes as he listened. He remembered singing it on that night before he went to Brighton. There had been cheers and screams. He had been in a mood of excitement, almost as if he'd been drugged. The whole scene flashed back to him as he sat listening.

The record stopped, and he looked down to his hands on the table before him. He thought of the complicated series of dreams he'd had the night before. He had slept badly, fitfully. In his dream he had been alone, wandering in London. The streets had seemed to be deserted. Everything had happened quickly, flashing in his mind from one scene to another. He had seen Carol walking in front of him on the other side of the street. They had come to Piccadilly. The flashing neon lights had blinded him; the large red Coca-Cola advert and the headlights of all the stationary traffic had seemed to shine in his eyes so that he could hardly see. He had looked around for Carol. She had been ahead of him still, about fifty yards away from him. He had looked around him at the lights and the adverts. Then suddenly everything had begun to come to life. The lights had suddenly begun to move, to come alive. Carol had screamed. The whole dream had turned suddenly into a nightmare. It was the nightmare of his monster. Everything seemed to change. They were not in London at all. The lights and the headlights were the monster. It was shapeless, formless, as always. He could not describe it, could not remember it. His mind retained only the impression, only the idea of it as a living, existing being. It had seemed evil, horrible. Sitting there in the café, the memory created shivers running down his spine. Carol had run from it, back across the empty void of his dream, away from the monster. Then suddenly she had been caught in it. The whole world had seemed to erupt into darkness. Chris had felt a sensation of falling, tumbling, downward, downward. The world had crashed into the holocaust. All time fled before him in the disaster as he fell, downward, downward, downward. Then, unexpectedly, he seemed to hit the ground. He could remember the jolt of it even now. Carol had vanished. He tried to stand up, but he felt he was too weak. His legs refused to support him. He suddenly seemed to realize that the whole thing was a dream. He realized suddenly that if he wanted to, he could merely open his eyes, and the whole thing would be over. He got to his feet. He seemed to be surrounded by pillars, a palisade of sticks. Above him he saw the formless outline of the monster. It seemed to be reaching down for him, approaching him. He turned to run. His legs felt weak still. He ran faster. Below him his legs felt as though they would collapse. He ran to the edge of the palisade until he found himself trapped. He turned back toward the thing that was following him. The feeling of frantic fear spread through the whole of his body. The monster came nearer. Then suddenly he woke up.

Lying there in bed, he found himself sweating. Sitting in the café, he was sweating still. The memory of his dream terrified him. He looked around him at the friendly, unknowing faces. His eyes darted from person to person. Suddenly he realized where he was. The dream was over. He had been reliving it, but now it was over. He looked down at his Coca-Cola. His cigarette end had burned away. He lit another cigarette and finished his drink.

People pushed through the crowds at the doorway to get to the jukebox or to the cigarette machines near to the counter. Chris watched them. Youthful, swearing, searching, aimless. There was an outward air of resolve about them, resolve toward the lives that they were leading, the nicotine that they were addicted to, the Coke or the foul coffee that they were drinking. What did they do with themselves all day? Did they just wander the streets of Soho from café to café, the way Chris had done over the last month? Or were they contented, responsible, respectable?

Chris thought to himself suddenly, This small hint of madness, of insanity, in me, is it just mine or is it a reflection of the general insanity of the whole generation? Do they all feel this sudden futility, or is it just me? His head reeled suddenly as he inhaled the cigarette smoke. Why do they just stand there? Why doesn't one of them say something? Why can't one of us get up and shout suddenly? Why can't we make something happen?

It's useless, it's pointless. Sitting here like this, we're just drifting onward into the same complacency as our fucking parents. Why doesn't one of us just shout out from the rooftops, "The world doesn't exist because I don't accept it. Conceptions don't exist because I refute them. The café doesn't exist because I refuse to believe in it"?

He flopped forward against the table. Outside the sun was shining. He squashed his cigarette in the ashtray and got up suddenly from his chair. He felt safe again out in the sun. There was security in the daylight. His nightmares came only in the darkness. He was safe in the sun.

At Piccadilly he stood for a minute, his eyes on the traffic. The hurly-burly of cars and buses swept past him like a whirlwind. Activity. Movement.

He crossed to Eros, the Island of Love. There was a sense of belonging for him here, among the hippies and the poets and the artists, sitting on the steps below the statue.

Some girl smiled at him. He crossed to the other side of Piccadilly and walked slowly again toward Trafalgar Square. What day was it? He tried to remember. It was about the middle of the week. Tuesday or Wednesday . . . He thought, What day did Pete die? What time was it? It was early in the morning. All the time he was lying there, I was sleeping. All the time I was asleep, Pete was lying there dead. The outline of Nelson's Column surged toward him, standing high above the square. All the time I was sleeping, Pete's body was lying there on the floor, dead.

On a bench in Trafalgar Square he fell into an interrupted, uneasy sleep. When he woke up for the last time, it was early afternoon. He shook himself to wake himself up. The memory of where he was flashed back to him. His eyes looked tired, dopey still. He felt automatically in the pockets of his parka for a cigarette. When he lit it, it tasted of bitter sulfur at the back of his mouth. Pigeons lingered at his feet. A policeman passed him. He rubbed his eyes. There was an aching in his head. He had a headache, a dull pain in his right temple. It hurt him when he moved his head. He felt as if he were only half awake, he felt incapable of waking up properly.

The sounds of traffic rose about his ears. Am I awake or asleep? Am I really here or is it a dream?

He forced himself to stand up and to walk to one of the fountains, where he could stand in the spray of the water and clear his head. Two boys darted around the fountain, splashing water over two girls.

Chris wasted the afternoon away. By the time five o'clock came, the day had spun itself away into a half-real dream. He talked to no one, did nothing.

The rush hour seemed to descend on London like an unexpected dust storm. Chris made his way back toward Chelsea. The tubes were crowded, and so he walked.

He said to himself as he walked, "There is an annonymity about London. But paradise isn't here. London is too close to me. Paradise isn't here." He spoke the words softly, but aloud. His hands were in the pockets of his parka, and he looked filthy and disreputable. People watched him as he walked. An old man sniffed as he passed him at a bus stop.

It was amusing to Chris somehow. He laughed to himself. He said, "It's the first time I've laughed in about two weeks."

He arrived at the flat and went in.

"Hi ya, Spud."

Spud looked up. "Hi, Chris."

Lorraine was borrowing a shilling for the gas meter, and Carol was out.

Spud said, "You fancy coming out to a pub some-where tonight?"

"Yeah, if ya like."

They sat for a while in silence. Chris didn't feel any need to talk. He sat there, silent. Sitting there on the bed, he had a sudden fleeting memory of the dream he'd had the night before. He felt scared suddenly. Lorraine came back again. She heated a tin of soup, and they sat eating it. When they'd finished, Lorraine threw the plates down into the sink with the rest of their washing up.

"The radio's packed up. We'll have to get some new batteries."

"The fucking thing oscillates too much. It needs a new loudspeaker."

Lorraine put on the record player. She put on a Stones L.P., and the sound of the record filled the whole flat. Lorraine boiled some water and made cof-fee. They spread themselves out around the room, Spud in a chair and Chris and Lorraine sitting on the bed.

Lorraine said, "Carol wanted to see you, Chris."

"What for?"

"Her father came down here. He was looking for her. He knows it was you who helped her leave home. He came here, and Spud got rid of him."

"Oh, God." Chris pushed his hand over the sweat of his face. The pain of his headache seemed to hit him again, the dull throbbing on the right side of his head. "He hasn't seen her, has he?"

"It's all right. He hasn't seen her." Spud was leaning forward, his elbows resting on his knees. "I told him I didn't know anything about it. I told him you'd moved out of here months ago, and I was living here with Lorraine." Spud looked up from underneath his mass of hair. "He started getting mad and trying to start a fight, so I hit him. I said if he didn't fuck off, I'd call the police."

"What happened then?"

"He went. He said to tell her he'd be back for her. I made out I still didn't know anything about it and told him to piss off."

"He was a right bastard, Chris. Spud told Carol about it when she got in, and she was scared stiff. She started crying. She's scared of what he'll do to her. If he finds her, he can tell the police, and she'll have to go back home with him. He'd make her life hell. Like I said, she's terrified of him. He's even worse than my old man. Christ, that's saying something." Lorraine looked as if she wanted to say something more but didn't know how to say it.

Chris said, "What did she want to see me for?"

Spud looked down at his feet then up again at Lorraine. He sipped at his coffee. He had difficulty in saying it. He said, "She didn't want you to worry about her, Chris."

"What d'ya mean, worry about her?" Chris fought against the pain in his head. He said, "I don't understand what you're talking about. I feel like I'm dreaming again. Everything that happens to me seems to feel like a dream. What's the matter, Spud?"

Spud sat up and looked at him. "Look, Chris, we all sat down in the other room, and we talked about what we thought we ought to do. The girl was broke, so I've lent her some money."

"What the hell for?" A wave of terror came over him. The memory of his dream raced again through his mind.

"She's having an abortion, Chris."

IV

Chris walked through the drizzle of Chelsea. The rain had started about ten minutes ago. A sort of desperation raced through him. He couldn't go out with Spud and Lorraine now. He had to be by himself. The words sounded corny now to him as he thought of them. But they're true, he thought to himself. It's true. I've killed Pete already, and now perhaps I'm gonna be responsible for killing Carol.

He tried to bring the memory of Carol's face back into his mind. I can't even remember her. My memory's killing her already. I can't even remember what she looks like. A shiver of terror went through him.

Why can't I remember her? I can't remember anything. My God, I can't— He reached a road. Traffic stood waiting at the traffic lights. He crossed over to the opposite pavement. The lights of a pub beckoned him on the corner of the street.

What can I remember about her? Nothing. I can't remember her at all. I'm going mad. Why can't I remember her? What's happening to me? My whole memory's going mad. Everything is haywire. I can't remember her face, can't remember her hair, can't remember her mouth, can't remember her eyes, can't remember anything. Where am I going? What am I doing? It's nighttime. If I sleep, then I'll dream again. How can I dream? I'm too scared of what I'll see in it. How can I sleep if I'm too scared to dream? How can I live if I'm too scared to fucking sleep?

He looked around him along the streets. People passed him, going in and out of the pub. He moved back, leaned himself against the pub wall. A girl came up to him, stood there as if she were trying to recognize him, expecting him to recognize her. Chris did not seem even to see her.

She said, "You're Chris Plater."

He saw her for the first time. "Yeah. What—"

"I'm Terry. I saw you once before. At Napoleon's."

Chris blinked. She was short, and he looked down at her. He didn't seem to understand what she was talking about for a while. The names didn't seem to register in his brain. Terry looked as if she had been crying. She said, "You look like you're ill. Come in here and get a drink. Christ, you look like—"

She led him toward the door of the pub. He made an effort to pull himself together. The pub was crowded, people standing everywhere. They went through into the other bar, where it wasn't so noisy.

They sat down. Terry looked over at the bar. Chris said, "You want something to drink? I just want cider. My head's aching."

"I'll get them." Terry stood up. She said, "You look like you need to sit down for a while."

She went to get the drinks. Chris rubbed his eyes and tried to shake his head. The pain of his headache seemed to spread through the whole of his body. He looked up to Terry as she came back across the room.

"What are you doing around here?" Chris propped up his head with his fingers under his chin.

"I live around here." She brushed back her hair away from her eyes. "I was only walking. I was thinking about Napoleon."

Chris was going to say, "What'd you say your name was again?" but he stopped himself just in time. His mind was operating on two different levels, flipping backward and forward from Pete and Carol to the things that were going on around him. There was a sort of mental block. He didn't seem to be able to remember things.

She's the girl who came to see Napoleon. The girl I had to go down and get rid of. Why's it so difficult for me to remember her? What is there to remember? Nothing. But I feel like remembering things is such a fucking effort suddenly. Not only about her, but about everyone. He clapped his hands again over his eyes. Terry looked at him, not understanding his exhaustion, his terror.

He moved away his hands.

She said, "I've only ever seen you on television before. Apart from the time at Napoleon's." She looked over at him and tried to smile. Then suddenly she lowered her head, and she started crying.

"What's the matter? Christ, what you crying for?"

She rubbed her face against the sleeve of her jacket and swore as she did so. "Nap's been arrested. I've been trying to see him since early last night, but they won't let me. Every time I go there, they tell me I can't see him—"

"What d'ya mean, arrested? What—what's he been fucking arrested for?"

She stopped crying again almost immediately. "There was a rally in Trafalgar Square. Anarchists and C.N.D. Napoleon got arrested."

Chris collapsed in his chair. For a long moment he was completely unaware of the girl's existence. His eyes clenched tight, and his body seemed to be shaking. He pushed his flesh hard against the back of his chair.

The wood bit through his parka and into his back. He wanted to scream, or shout, or yell, and yet he felt utterly exhausted. He felt totally incapable even of moving, and yet he felt that he couldn't bear to stay still. The sounds around him were empty, intolerable. His brain refused to take anything more in. His mind felt like the mainspring of a watch, winding up rapidly to the point where it seemed it must break.

"Police," he said.

"Cops.

"Sex.

"Crabs.

"Poisons.

"Filth.

"Lies."

She looked at him in astonishment. He was staring at the big, blue Turkish ring he'd been given by Carol. He seemed to be miles away, wrapped in his own thoughts. He took the ring off quickly. His fingers shook. He said, "Give this to Napoleon for me."

"Why?"

"Just give it to him. I don't want it. Give it to him."

"Are ya drunk?" she said.

"Drunk? Man, I'm dead. Shadows. Moonlight. Broken bottles. Two-dimensional pulse beats. Fish. Napoleon. You. Oh, God." His voice collapsed.

She clasped her fingers tight around the ring. "They put Napoleon in a van. They took him to West End

Central." Her voice was almost hysterical. For a moment she was near to crying again.

Chris said, "They never charged him?"

"They've got him in a cell. They told me that when I went to try and see him."

"Are ya in love with him?"

"Who?"

"Nap, I mean."

"No . . . well I don't know. I love lots of people."

"Everybody. Nobody. I'm sick. Nap's sick. Spud's sick. Lorraine's sick. You're sick. The queen's sick. The prime minister's sick. Everyone's sick. No one can fight it. The old generation's dying. The new generation's being dragged into the whirlpool with it. The ones who fight get arrested and dragged to some police station. The others stand there up to their necks in the quagmire and just decay, not even realizing what's happening."

"Happening where?" She stared at him. The tears were drying now around her eyes. People were watching them. She felt as if she were caught up somehow in some sort of desperate, meaningful piece of drunken self-revelation. The change in him since the first time she'd seen him was enormous. She drank down the whole of her vodka, and it made her feel slightly drunk herself. The scene they were acting was insanely mad. Yet it didn't seem to matter.

"Happening where?"

193

"Happening everywhere. Here. The house down the road. I'm blinding myself by thinking I can see it, but I can't. It's too big to ever see all of it. So I'm dragged down in it too. God. D'you believe in God? Jesus Christ?"

"Yeah, I suppose I do sometimes. I ain't sure about religion yet. I don't know."

"Well, you show me your Son of God, you show me your Jesus Christ, the man who came to save the world. And I'll take his trousers down for you. And underneath them you'll find two balls and a pink prick just the same as everyone else. Came to save the world? Next time perhaps he can make a better job of it. Next time perhaps he can treat us like equals. Everyone's equal in heaven? Yeah, everyone except him and that old man of his. Everyone's equal, and them two are more equal than others."

The bar began to get more crowded. Chris talked as if he were unaware of everyone. He finished his drink, and they got some more. This time they went to the bar together. Terry picked up the two drinks. The barman handed the change to Chris.

"Change."

Chris stared at him, unhearing.

"Change."

"What . . . change?" He blinked, picked up the change suddenly and went back across to the table.

He put down the change, and he looked into Terry's face. She looked up, and she caught his eyes.

"What's the matter?" she said quickly.

He didn't speak for a minute. "I gotta go," he said.

"Where? What for?"

His eyes looked stony, covered with a glaze. "I gotta go. I gotta go."

He ran out into the street. He ran straight out into the road and fled. What's happening to me? What was I doing there? I'm dreaming. Can I be dreaming? Or was I, for a minute, insane? Napoleon. Something happened to Napoleon. Everything blank. Can't remember what I was doing. Alternate periods of sanity and madness. No, insanity does not exist. Doesn't it? Does it? What's happening to me? Is the fight beginning? Sanity versus madness. Oh, fuck. Fuck it all, fuck it all, fuck it all, fuck it all, fuck it all, fuck it all. What can I do?

He stopped a hundred yards from the tube station. Fuck, fuck, fuck, fuck, fuck, fuck, fuck. What'm I doing? Catch a tube? Make for Piccadilly, Soho? Soho is safe for me. Soho is safe.

He caught the tube. Coming out into the streets again at Piccadilly, the cold air seemed to hit him, smacking against his face like a flat, gigantic fist. He walked the pavements into Soho. The Soho people moved, detached, all about him, each of them lost in his own separate world. The two young boys—provincial and dressed to disguise this fact—come to see the great city. The boy who sold dope. The girl called Angelina who knew everybody.

Chris knew them all, saw them all, accepted them all, dismissed them all, for he was one of them himself. He didn't need to see them with his eyes or react to them with his mind. He passed them on the street, and they passed him. Everything was automatic. When he was the provincial boys' age, he would have challenged the two of them to a fight, he and his cousin, during late afternoon in Trafalgar Square. The boy who sold dope he knew because he had bought dope himself. The girl called Angelina he knew because there were girls called Angelina everywhere.

Chris wrapped himself in his parka and walked with his eyes watching everything, seeing nothing. For a while he just walked. He walked along Wardour Street, turned off into a side street and then cut off through another semi-alleyway until he was lost. By a closed doorway a Negro woman stood, very large, her lips painted pink. They glanced at each other momentarily, a look of acknowledgment, and then they both returned their glances to within themselves.

Chris walked with a look of terror. He went into a pub and got himself partially drunk. He sat there, staring at nothing, his head most of the time flopped forward onto the table and turned to one side to face the wall. When he left that pub, he walked again and went into another one, and after that another. He got himself sloshed. As he walked, the night air made his drunkenness seem even more exaggerated, even more intense.

But somehow, getting drunk wasn't enough. Chris was trying to tranquilize his mind, to put it to sleep so that he would cease having to think. But this time it wasn't enough. Parts of his body were sleeping, perhaps, but not his brain. His thoughts twisted still within his mind, drunkenly perhaps but present all the same.

Carol is having an abortion. Nap is in prison. Pete's dead. What is there left? What more could happen now? The ceiling could fall, perhaps. The sky could crumble into the dust. The mountains could all erupt and explode. The seas could sweep over us all and drown us. The bomb could go off now and kill us. But it wouldn't matter. Not one fucking piece of it all would ever matter. The world's falling around my ears. Are all these things happening, have these things happened, or am I just imagining them?

Visions. I see a great vision. Crowds with placards. Scuffles. The police. Somehow it's connected with me. How, I don't know. Visions drift. Images fade. Everything dies, disappears. Why can't I remember? Why can't I remember? Something happened to me tonight, something broke. Was I conscious of what I was doing, or was I mad? Is that the test, consciousness? Or can you be mad and still be conscious of all your actions?

Yes, of course you fucking can. There's an aching in my head. I'm sloshed. I feel lightheaded, but I've got a headache at the same time.

Bones.

Skin.

Mud.

Heat.

His eyes almost sparkled. He was lost still as he walked, but he didn't even bother to look where he was going. His mind was everything. The part of it that was in control of his body was now forgotten.

People. Around you, all around you. Are they like you or are they different? Different? No. Things are the same. Lights. Colors. Neon blues. Reds and greens. What's happened to Napoleon? I heard he was arrested. I don't remember how I heard it. Someone told me. I don't remember who. I don't remember. I don't remember. Why can't I remember things? Is there no memory? Where is my memory? Where is my memory? Things are lost in me. I feel myself disconnected from the world. There is a seed of disease in me. The seed is rotting at my memory. The seed of the world's insanity. The universal insanity. Insanity of the world. I remember Tambourine Man. Tambourine Man. It seems a long time. A long time since I heard you. My paradise gets difficult, Dylan. Everything gets harder. I feel all the time that the road is steeper. But I am mad,

Dylan, and you are sane. You know all these things already.

Tambourine.

Fire.

House.

Door.

Man.

Rat.

He stopped walking. The car noises finally awakened him. He looked around him. He recognized the place but was still hardly aware of where he was. Along the road there was a group of clubs. The mods walked past him toward them, going for the late night session until three or four o'clock the next morning. Chris walked in the same direction. Someone bumped into him in the street. The boy moved away from him again quickly, not wishing to start anything. Both of them remained silent, no apologies.

There were three or four sailors on the other side of the road. Chris saw them without noticing. He walked until he got to another pub. The time was about a quarter past ten. Chris almost walked straight on past the pub because he didn't see it. The barman told Chris he looked as if he'd had too much to drink already. Chris swore at him. Eventually the man sold him a pint of mild, and Chris stumbled to the other side of the room.

He sat, and his mind spun. His fingers tapped irritably, absently, on the table. He lounged back in his chair, and eventually his eyes fell lightly shut. He was not asleep, but suddenly his body had felt exhausted, and he had had to rest. He opened his eyes to sip at his beer and then lounged back again, grating the back of the chair against the wall. Some of the sailors came into the pub and sat quite near to him. Some of them were with girls, others sat unaccompanied. Chris paid no attention, did not notice them.

He leaned forward in his chair and lit himself a cigarette, having a drink of his beer as he did so. He glanced up absently at the figures standing by the bar. One of them had his back to Chris. He was quite young, only about a year older than Chris was himself. He wore dirty black corduroy trousers and a brown-colored jacket and had quite long, dark-colored, untidy hair.

The boy turned around. Chris stared at him. He knew him from somewhere. He couldn't think where. Chris fought against his blocked memory, trying to remember. It was the hitchhiker, the boy they'd met going down to Brighton before the tour of Scotland. Spud had been there, and Lorraine. The boy's name was something like—Chris struggled. Mark, it was Mark.

Mark saw Chris looking at him. Realization seemed to dawn over his face almost immediately. He came over and stood by Chris' chair.

"It's Chris Plater, isn't it? We met before, d'ya remember?"

Mark sat, and they began to talk. Most of the talking was done by Mark. Chris seemed unable to concentrate, and his mind wandered, but he nodded here and there in Mark's conversation because he was glad suddenly to have someone to sit with.

Mark seemed to notice the strangeness in his expression, the inattentiveness. He watched Chris all the time, seemed to watch his eyes and his hands. Chris didn't appear to notice this, but Mark watched very carefully.

"How you gonna get home?" Mark said. "You'd be too drunk to get home by yourself."

"I don't wanna go home yet. My friend's in a police cell. I told ya, I'm not going home. I'll sleep out somewhere."

"You want to carry on drinking?"

"I s'pose so, yeah. Why?"

"There's a party later on, back at this place where I live in Wandsworth. Why don't you come there?"

V

Chris agreed, and they went to Wandsworth. They walked through the rain from the tube station.

Mark said, "The buses around here are useless. We could probably wait half an hour before the right one comes along. We might as well walk. Either way we're gonna get drenched."

Chris left his parka hanging open and flapping at his sides. The rain didn't bother him at all. They reached Allfarthing Lane.

"Down here." Mark led the way down the steps to the basement. He found the front-door key from somewhere behind the dustbins, and they went in. They were in a passage, lights on everywhere.

Chris thought, Behind it all, behind the mechanisms and the twisting of life, there stands the great and immortal magician. The genius, devil figure of evil, hiding always on the darkest crest of the rainbow, manipulating constantly the mental disintegration of the world, cowering beneath the veil of his own cloak as he builds and expands his powers, waiting always in the background, deep at the bottom of the deepest ocean, as his creeping plague of madness takes its grip on the world. . . .

"Chuck your coat somewhere. It doesn't matter where you put things. The place is a mess anyway." Mark pushed open a door right at the beginning of the passage. "That's the bog. Bardino lives in a room upstairs. The rest of us sleep out down here."

The whole basement was a maze of passages and rooms. A girl was standing, making coffee in the kitchen. Chris said, "Who's Bardino?"

"Olson. You met him at Brighton."

The girl glanced around at them.

"Hi, Elisabeth."

"Hi, Mark. Who you got with you?"

"This is Chris Plater. I told you about him. We've been drinking. Can you give us some coffee?"

"Yeah, sure." Elisabeth spooned coffee into chipped cups and came over to sit on the edge of the table. "You're staying for the party?" she said to Chris.

"I ain't sure."

"Mark said he got a lift from you down to Brighton."

He flopped against the table and sat down to one side of her. "Yeah."

She said, "How bad is it? You look pretty drunk."

"I am. I'll be all right. Give me a minute sitting down."

Mark said, "I'll do the coffee." The kettle had boiled, and he moved across to pour out the water. Someone came in through the door.

"Make mine white, will you, Mark?" He walked straight through the kitchen and out to the toilet.

Elisabeth said, "That's Simon."

Simon came back, and they were introduced. Simon looked shy, but he talked almost endlessly, losing every trace of his self-consciousness as he got more and more excited.

Chris thought to himself, These people are all religious maniacs. And yet to look at them, they all seem completely sane. What does that mean? Does it mean that I'm even further gone than I thought? Does it mean that I'm even further gone than they are? Or does it mean that they're really not mad at all?

The sound of folk music came suddenly from one of the other rooms. They took their coffee and went through into the next room opposite them across the corridor. The room was almost bare of furniture, a camp bed and a table standing on one side of the room, a record player and a pile of records near the door. Someone sat facing the record player, leaning forward over a newspaper spread on the floor in front of him. He got out a knife and a cigarette, shredded the cigarette, added mirijuana and rolled it in a new paper and then lit it. The record was Joan Baez. The sound of her voice floated, quiet but piercing, through the whole room.

Chris stood by the door. The marijuana was passed from hand to hand, and Simon returned to the kitchen, brought back some wine and poured it into their coffee. The wine made the coffee almost undrinkable. Chris was finding it difficult to stand up. He fell against Elisabeth and then managed to pull himself back into an upright position for a moment, leaning against the frame of the doorway.

Elisabeth said, "Christ, you're drunker than I thought. You better come and sit down."

Chris tried to move forward into the room. He stumbled, and Elisabeth grabbed his arm to try to steady him.

He collapsed onto the floor, hit his knee, and then fell forward against his spilled coffee on the bare floorboards. He lay there, and the room spun around him. He felt as if he were incapable of moving. The party went on practically as if nothing had happened. He looked up again at the room spinning around him and then closed his eyes. It was a sort of drunken half-sleep lasting almost ten minutes. At first Chris was aware of Elisabeth trying to help him stand up again, and then he lost consciousness.

Before the unconsciousness left him, he dreamed. He was at a party somewhere. He was sitting on the ground with someone and talking. At first he didn't know where he was, but then things became clearer to him. He realized he was on the beach at Brighton again, talking to Pat. It was the night that they had all piled into the van and driven down to Brighton. The scene repeated itself exactly in his mind. He saw Kathy, lying there next to Mark and shivering. Lorraine sat there with her leather jacket spread out on the sand, not seeming to feel the cold at all. He heard his own voice, talking again about Dylan's "Mr. Tambourine Man": "Dylan doesn't believe in paradise, so he's trying to create a paradise of his own. The boy who sings 'Mr. Tambourine Man' is trying to find that paradise. Dylan says . . ." He heard himself repeating the words of the song again, over and over.

He saw Spud sitting there with the reefer to his lips, saw the guitar resting in front of him on the sand, saw the reefer between his own fingers, looked up suddenly to the sea. Suddenly his dream had changed. What was it that he could see moving on the waves? Was there something there, or was it imagination? Something was coming out of the sea, something was coming toward them.

Chris moved suddenly on the hard wooden floor. In his dream he was shouting, screaming. For a moment he was fully awake again. Then he went back to semiconsciousness. Chris wasn't sure whether he was dreaming or not. It had all the qualities of a dream, yet he felt he was awake still. He could feel the floorboards beneath him, hear the record player.

He was back in the dressing room in Dundee, talking to Pete. The order of things was confused. The dream made hardly any visual impression on him at all. He could hear the voices again, his and Pete's, but the words were taken out of order, out of context. Pete said, "But you know what you're looking for," and he said, "Yeah, I know what I'm looking for. I'm looking for Mr. Tambourine Man's paradise. I'm looking for the distant horizon just like everyone else."

Then suddenly they were talking about suicide. They talked about suicide for a long time, and then

206

Pete said, "But you don't really believe that." Chris heard his own voice saying, "Why?" and Pete said, "Because if you did, you'd shoot yourself."

Suddenly the picture of Pete flashed before his eyes, Pete lying dead on the floor in the hotel in Edinburgh. He writhed again on the floor. Something seemed to force itself into his mind, take command of all his attention. He looked up, and the eyes of Olson stared down at him from the sky. Elisabeth laughed. He heard her saying, "Christ, you'd better not do anymore drinking tonight. I'll make you some black coffee."

Mark helped him up. There was a strangeness about them all. He tried to shake the memories he'd just had out of his mind. Olson stood back. He looked at Mark and then at Simon. Behind Olson, Chris could see Mary.

Olson made a gesture of welcome, holding out his hand. "We've met before."

Chris took hold of the hand. His mind was spinning. He looked about him as if he didn't know where he was. An old blanket had been drawn across the window as a curtain. Apart from that, everything was the same as before. He shook Olson's hand and was aware of a great surge of personality seeming to hit him like a physical force. He opened his eyes wide. Olson watched him. He was aware of the blazing eyes staring deep into his own, into his face.

Olson smiled and turned away. Chris noticed a sudden quietness come over the whole room. Simon put down his bottle of wine on the table. Chris struggled with the confusion of his mind. His mind revolted against the thoughts that his memory had dredged back to him. He shut Pete and Lorraine and Spud and Kathy and Pat out of his mind. A wave of drunken nausea came over him. Tambourine Man. Tambourine Man. The poem of salvation. The hazy devil figure with his red eyes. And Dylan's imperial music maker. Where are they all? Their eyes, hypnotic and alive. Tambourine Man, slumbering in some distant subconscious.

How much further is it to Tambourine Man's paradise? Boy, you'll never make it. Give up now. You're finished. Or have you perhaps arrived there already? How will you know when you arrive? Perhaps this is it. Perhaps you're on the edge of it already. Have you got the strength to carry on, get to the center? Give up now, and it's worse than if you never started. You can't go back, and you're not strong enough to go forward.

What do the eyes mean? The eyes are the monster. Bardino's eyes. Are they pushing you forward or holding you back? How can you look at them? Concentrate, you must concentrate.

Elisabeth came back again, and it brought him back to his senses. He realized he was more or less alone in the center of the room. The others were sitting in a sort of loose semicircle around the walls. Elisabeth sat him down near to the table, and he drank the black coffee with her. Olson sat at the table, eating. Simon sat at the table with him. All the others were on the floor. Everyone carried on as they had before Olson had entered, but they were quieter, as if not wishing to talk too loudly in case he should want to speak.

A boy was lying drunkenly on the floor, half behind the open door, out of Olson's vision. There were some loaves of bread and some fruit. It was like a sort of evening meal. Elisabeth's eyes seemed to flit backward and forward from Olson to Chris. Chris looked over to Olson, too. He sat eating, his face old against all the young faces around him, his hair short and neat, his eyes and the lines across his forehead looking deep and shadowy in the artificial light. Somewhere someone laughed. Elisabeth didn't seem to hear it. She was looking still at Olson. She said to Chris, half turning, "He is the greatest man in the world, and someday they'll kill him."

Olson looked up from his meal and glanced across at them. He couldn't have heard her because she'd been whispering, but he stared straight at them, any expression on his face lost in the reflection of the lights and in the shadows they cast on his face. Chris was oblivious to it all. He withdrew again into his thoughts. He felt a great difficulty in controlling his own mind. A sudden panic came to him. What if I'm trapped here with these lunatics for the rest of eternity? Bardino, you're reading into my mind, hypnotizing me, stealing my brain. I can feel your fingers digging into the nerve cells of my brain, fighting my independence, stealing my reasoning.

From inside his mind he imagined he heard a voice answering him. I am the Bardino, the eternal, the lord of all things. Surrender yourself to me. Look into my eyes.

You can't control me. My brain defies you. I resist you. You are fighting for my mind. The words, the pain. I cannot listen to you. The eyes are the monster. The monster is the nonentity, the embodiment of evil, hidden in simplicity, controlling everything. You're invading my mind. Your fingers are ice, dissecting me, raping my brain.

I am the Bardino.

The feeling of invasion. What's happening to me? You're freezing me. I can't move, can't control my body anymore, my thoughts. What are you doing to me? Why am I feeling like this? Why can't I scream? Why can't I shout out at you? Why can't somebody help me? All of them. They can hear us. They can see you attacking me, mesmerizing me. Your eyes staring through into the back of my brain. Why can't they help me? Why can't they see? What's the matter with us all? You are controlling everyone, willing them to help you, to hold me down, to pin my arms and my legs. No one helps, no one moves. The world is watching you, gripped in your hands, obeying you, resisting but being broken, beaten. No one can move. Your will impedes them, spreading like a patch of darkness. The nighttime empire, encircling humanity, enveloping the sun as it reaches the dawn, strangling the sunsets of my mind as I look into your eyes.

I am the Bardino. Why won't you surrender to me? My powers could crush you in one swoop. Your brain is difficult, too confused. I am all-powerful, all-controlling. You must listen to me. I am the Bardino. You must obey me. You cannot defy me. You must allow your brain to sleep. Release the confusion of your mind. I can read it, all of it. Your mind is distorted. It is impossible for you to comprehend me, but you must sleep. I am the lord of life and the lord of death. You must relax. It is impossible for me to penetrate fully into your mind. You are a good subject, and yet you are confused. Your mind is a muddle. You must look into my face. You must relax.

Chris struggled against the voice inside his brain. He saw the vision in front of his eyes. Olson standing in front of him. The others in complete obedience. Olson's hand stretched out toward his head. The touch of Olson's hand. Your hand is paralyzing me. I can't move. I can't move. He saw himself shouting now. Olson's eyes staring at him, nothing more than Olson's eyes. Why do you want to invade me? Why can't I move? Why can't I think? Everything is painful. My head is breaking. My mind is cut. I feel your knife in it, your fingers, probing it, turning it over, fighting to control me, fighting to control me, fighting to control me, fighting to control me. . . .

His brain was filled with shouting, tense, explosive. The answering voice was screaming at him, screaming, screaming, screaming. I am the Bardino. I am the Bardino. I am the Bardino. I am the Bardino. The Bardino. The Bardino.

He saw himself standing. You cannot control me. Your fingers cannot hurt me. My madness protects me. My madness defends me against you. I can defy you. I can resist you. Your fingers burn against my insanity, your eyes blaze against my wall of flaming madness. Your powers creep against an unknown void.

The Bardino. The Bardino. The Bardino. The Bardino. He saw Bardino's eyes as if they were twin blazing moons. He saw himself standing, Olson before him. The eyes pierced at his brain. He could feel it again. The pain upon his forehead. The sudden physical shock of contact. He could feel his own body pinned again where he stood. In the vision he tried to scream again but couldn't. He tried to run, move. He saw the power in Olson's face.

Suddenly he was free. He was awake. He could move again. His hands were at Olson's neck. His fingers were digging deep. He screamed and yelled as loud as he could. His feet kicked, his hands dug, deeper,

deeper. Everything happened so fast, so quickly. His eyes were on Olson's. Suddenly there was a shock, like electricity running through his body. He was thrown against the door. He hit his head against the wall. He reeled and ached in every corner of his body.

Things became confused. He turned, terrified, ran toward the kitchen. His coat seemed almost to jump up into his hands from where he'd left it. He remembered climbing the steps up from the basement and onto the road. The terror raced still through his body. He was caught up for a moment irretrievably in his thoughts. He was completely unaware of where he was or what was happening.

When he realized finally where he was, he was in the rain, walking in Wandsworth in the early hours of the morning. The rain hit him in his face. Car headlights blazed in his eyes.

VI

Did I dream it? Was it just in my mind? Or did it really happen?

The car turned a corner and disappeared. It was late. He walked on, through the streets. The rain hit him still, again and again, on his face. He lit a cigarette and smoked it as he walked, the rainwater making it wet and soggy. Another car approached and passed him slowly. On the other side of the road there was a large children's playground. He glanced across at it.

Was it really happening, or did I dream it? Am I dreaming now? No, I can't be. I'm awake. I'm alive. But was I awake just now? How did I get out here? What happened? Do I even know the difference between what happens in my day-dreams and what actually happens to me in reality?

He walked for a long time, not even thinking. Suddenly he said out loud, "The rain is beating against my soul, drowning my mind, listening to my words as I talk here to the wind, defining me mad." He held the cigarette end before his eyes. "My eyes are insane. The insanity shows in my eyes. But where is the paradise? Where is the paradise? Is it here? Is this the paradise I'm looking for, submerged somewhere in the caves and streets of Wandsworth?" He dropped the cigarette end onto the wet pavement. "Am I mad? What's madness, anyway? I can't remember anything. Who am I? I'm lost. I don't know who I am, where I'm going to, what I'm doing."

He pulled the hood of his parka up over his head and did up the buttons. He pushed his hands into his pockets. It was cold, wet. He walked directionlessly for almost three quarters of an hour. He found himself at Putney Bridge and crossed it into Fulham. He stood on the bridge, shivering, as he lit another cigarette. He held the match between the palms of his hands, watching it until it burned away. His hands felt sore and red with the cold and the rain. He began to walk again, almost parallel to the river. The rain poured harder. He walked on, and a policeman approached him from the other side of the road. Chris huddled himself down more snugly within his parka. The street was almost deserted. But for the sounds of the rain and their muffled footsteps, everything was silent.

"Just a minute."

"What?"

"Out a bit late, aren't you?" The policeman watched him from beneath his helmet. The rain ran off his plastic mackintosh.

"I don't know."

"Where you going?"

"I don't know."

"You been drinking?"

"No . . . yeah . . . I gotta go." He looked desperately up at the helmet. The policeman was tall. He seemed to be enormous.

"What's your name?"

"I—"

He didn't say anything. The policeman said, "You better come with me."

"I—" He felt a hand come down on his shoulder.

"We won't keep you long . . . perhaps."

"But I can't. I gotta—"

The grip tightened. Chris felt himself being led away. He shook himself free. "What ya taking me up here for?"

"Just checking."

"There's nothing wrong with me."

"We have to check. This time of night we don't know what you might be getting up to."

"There's nothing wrong with me, I said. I'm sane, I'm sane."

He moved back quickly. The policeman made a grab for him, surprised, and he ran. He ran back along the pavement, through the puddles and through the rain, past some hedges and then brick walls. He heard the policeman calling at him, chasing him. He came to a park backing onto the river. He knew the place. He had been here often with Lorraine. He ran on to the open land, the gate with the broken lock, the fence that had been broken down.

The sound of the policeman had vanished. He stopped for a moment and stood still. He listened for the policeman, but there was nothing. He went on into the park, breathing heavily. The rain dripped down from his hood and onto his face. He pushed back the hood and opened his parka. He wiped his face, caught his breath. He discovered a park bench and sat. His drunkenness swept back over him. He stretched out his feet, half sat, half lay, on the bench.

Where is the sea? Where can I drown myself? Where can I hide? Am I dead? Am I dreaming? Am I alive? Will I find you, Tambourine Man? Will I ever find you? Or will I just wander forever? All gods are false. All truths are lies. Will I find you, Tambourine Man? How many fags will I have to smoke, how much longer before I find you?

Where is the paradise? Where is the paradise?

Why can't I remember? Why can't I remember? Am I falling? Is my memory too clogged with nicotine to remember?

He forced himself to think of where he was, but he couldn't remember. For almost an hour he sat there, his mind a confusion of words and people that he could only half remember. The rain stopped, but his hair and his clothes and his face were wet and dripping. The hair hung flat down over his face and over his neck and over his ears. He felt the water run from it across his skin. He stood up and walked toward the river. The tide had gone out, and rubbish and pools of water were left amidst the sandy sludge on either side of the narrow Thames.

He watched the moon reflected on the water. He felt cold, and the wind blew at him strongly from across the river, but he ignored it. He tried to concentrate. His mind strayed from subject to subject, from half-forgotten memory to half-forgotten memory. He fixed his gaze on the reflection of the moon, watched its ripples in the moving water. But everything seemed unreal to him. As he stood there, he was not staring at the Thames at all but at something more distant, some vision or daydream in his mind. He began to talk to himself very softly, the words almost inaudible. The words made no sense, and as he said them he seemed to know that they didn't. He imagined that he was talking to someone, that someone else was there with him, standing there beside him.

He heard in his own mind the poem he had once written, "The Golden Realm of Dreams." He remembered it, word for word. He repeated it to himself, almost shouting it. The words seemed to come to him just as they had when he'd written it.

> Coming dewdrops of the morning
> break the only icy silence
> in the early hours of restlessness
> upon the mounded golden hilltop
> stretching 'cross the realm of dreams.
>
> I pray for sleep to save my body
> from the hick-land dome of reasoning
> —transport it to the hilltop
> in the wondrous realm of dreams
> where only freshly maidened water
> dares to flow the brimming river
> and just familied crabs of silence
> dare to speak their rhymeless word
> upon the printless silver paper
> in the golden realm of dreams.
> I have no ties to hold me back here
> in the outside world of thinking
> —have no broken chains of purpose
> —have no pancake of respect.

There are only foreign missiles
in this vast decaying shadow
where the fingers of night's empire
bring our only time of rest.
There are only foreign navies
I see only foreign armies
trampling through their distant forests
upon the track of mother war
—and yet I see the dreamland
hovering in the long-lost distance
and I pray for sleep to save me
from the pine-line time of killing
and transport me to the hilltop
in the golden realm of dreams.

A gust of wind blew his wet hair down into his eyes.
He looked up toward the sky. The wind blew at the
whole of his damp hair. He lit a cigarette. He said the
words again to himself. "And yet I see the dreamland.
And yet I see the dreamland." He hung his head, down,
down, until his forehead rested on the guardrail overlooking the river. "What's the point? What's the
point?"

It began to rain again. He stood there alone for nearly
an hour. A wave of nausea swept over him again. He
held onto the rail to steady himself, to stop himself falling.

Suddenly there was a noise. He stood listening. People talking. Two of them. Boy and girl. He turned
around. He could see the figures through the trees.

Both of them were wet, complaining about the rain. The girl wore a leather jacket. He could see her quite plainly. Her hair was long and brown. She wore tight, wet jeans. In her hand she held a wet cigarette.

They were coming toward him. He moved away quickly from the rail. What d'they want? What d'they want? He tried to keep out of their sight, but it was impossible. One of them saw him. There was a shout of surprise as he was first seen. The memory of the policeman came back to him. He shivered for a moment as he stood there in his terror.

Then he ran. He tore away through the rain. His feet almost slipped for a moment, and he ran on faster, imagining all the time the sound of the other four feet slipping behind him. A wave of sickness came over him, and he ran over the wet grass, tripped on something, felt himself falling, falling.

He heard the sound of footsteps. Chris looked up at the girl who stood before him, and then suddenly he passed out. He realized before he passed out that the girl was someone he remembered. A dim feeling of recognition stirred in his stifled mind. He realized, almost in his last second of consciousness, that the girl was Lorraine.

Chris awoke again for a second in the hospital bed. Standing over him were a nurse and a doctor. The doctor wore glasses and a gray suit.

The nurse was saying, "Yes, sir, they're outside."

"And Mr. Matthews admitted him?"

"Yes, sir."

"What did he say?" The doctor caught Chris' eye and noticed that he was awake. He smiled down at him and moved away with the nurse. Chris fell back into unconsciousness. The doctor and nurse stood talking for a moment in low voices at the foot of the bed.

The room was small and smelled of sheets. Doctor Stevenson walked to the door and out into the corridor, leaving the nurse sitting by the bed. He walked to the room where Spud and Lorraine were waiting at the end of the corridor. Spud was smoking heavily. Lorraine stood by the door, looking down toward Spud's lowered head.

She turned at the opening of the door.

Doctor Stevenson said, "I've just seen him. He's sleeping again. I think we should let him sleep for as long as possible."

He sat down on the edge of his desk. Spud handed Lorraine a cigarette. She said quickly, "What do you think's the matter with him?"

"At the moment, he's tired and he's drunk. That's all I know." The doctor took off his glasses and eased his eyes. "I want you to tell me everything strange that you've noticed about him in the last few months, going back as far as you can remember. How long has he been acting the way he acted tonight, and is there any reason that you know of why he could be doing it?'

"I don't know—"

"Has he been taking drugs?" The doctor's voice was friendly and helpful.

"Yes."

Spud said, "But he's been taking drugs since he was fifteen years old."

The doctor nodded. "When he works—is he happy when he's working, or does it tire him?"

"He likes working, but he seems to push himself too hard. He doesn't get enough rest, and then suddenly it all seems to catch up on him, and he feels completely exhausted."

Lorraine looked at Spud. He took her hand.

Stevenson said, "I want him to stay here for two weeks. He mustn't do any work at all. I think you ought to persuade him to agree to it. And then we'll see."

Lorraine nodded. Her hair was damp still, and her hands felt numb and cold. She leaned forward toward an ashtray and flicked the ash into it from the end of her cigarette.

VII

Two weeks later Chris went to Cramond Island. The weeks in hospital were sickening. He left on a Tuesday morning, took five pounds with him and hitchhiked north. When he got to Edinburgh it was late on Wednesday. He found Princes Street, walked to Leith and then down onto the front and along until he found the pipeline out to the island.

He lived on cigarettes and tins of soup. During the nights he slept in the blockhouse set apart at the south end of the island. In the mornings he woke up with the tide, threw his parka over his shoulders and climbed down onto the beach. He lit himself a fire, heated up his soup, and ate it quickly, sitting among the rocks and looking back toward the mainland. The wind blew from behind him, throwing out his hair toward the sea, and he sat there for hours, watching the yachts as they sailed past the island, or the Forth road bridge as it stood there, half hidden, against the sky.

Apart from Chris, the island was completely uninhabited. In the afternoons people would come across perhaps from the mainland for a couple of hours while the tide was out and it was possible to cross. Chris would go back to the balcony of the blockhouse out of their way or merely sit there on the beach and ignore them. Once a girl approached him, and they talked for hours, she in her broad Scots accent, he in his London south. They talked of war, peace, pop music and madness, heredity and sex. The girl didn't recognize Chris, and he was glad. She took him for just another hippie with nowhere else to go, and they talked until the tide had almost come in again, and she could only just get back out onto the mainland. Chris thought about her for the rest of the day. She reminded him of the two girls he'd met in Edinburgh before, during August. What were their names? What did they look like? He couldn't remember, couldn't remember anything. Everything about them had vanished. What was the use of memories? What was the use of anything? It didn't matter. Everything was lost to him now, anyway. He was happy after a fashion. His own mind was clearer, happier. That was all that mattered.

He sat smoking on the beach one day and wishing he'd brought his guitar. He sang "Mr. Tambourine Man" to the attentive waves. He'd been there for over a week. He didn't know what day it was, what time it was. For a whole week he'd sat thinking about nothing, resting his mind. He repeated the words he'd once said about "Mr. Tambourine Man": " 'Tambourine Man' is a search for peace. Dylan doesn't believe in paradise, so he's created a paradise of his own."

But how could you create a paradise? Even here he wasn't in paradise. No one could create a worldly paradise. What he needed to create was a paradise in his own mind. If you could do that, it wouldn't matter where you were, what air you breathed.

He took a gulp from the bottle of water at his side. When he'd first come, he'd bought himself five bottles of wine. When the wine was gone, he crossed quickly to the mainland and filled the bottles up with water. His mouth was dry because he'd been drinking so little, rationing himself. He gulped down almost a quarter of the bottle. His mind turned back to the girl who'd come to talk to him three days before. He wondered if she would come back. He had come here to get away from everyone, and yet talking to her had been good, refreshing. He waited on the beach all that day to see if she would come.

When all the tins of soup were finished, he came onto the beach every morning the same as before and sat by his fire, looking out to the sea. One afternoon he explored the island again. Everything was just the same as it had been before, when he'd explored the island with Pete and the two girls. He saw his own name written in chalk on the rotting walls, saw Pete's name and the scrawled messages. Donovan slept here. I Want to Meet a Bird. I Love Terry. Fuck King Billy. Yanks Go Home.

Chris walked around the island from hut to hut. The place was deserted. He wondered where everyone was. Where have all the hippies gone? Gone to prisons every one. He smiled to himself in his happiness and walked on. He stood at the north end of the island, where most of the gun mountings and blockhouses were. Below him was the hut where Donovan slept, a hut designed for war whose final use was as a shelter for Donovan Leitch—a pacifist. Chris smiled again. He started to laugh as he stood there on the rocks. The wind came to him straight off the sea. It was so strong that for a moment he could hardly stand up. He stood looking at the smaller, more built-up island across just to his left. Straight ahead of him there was Edinburgh, and right behind him there was Dunfermline. He turned around again and started to walk back. The island road was narrow and overgrown with weeds. The grass and bushes had grown tall on either side of the road, and mice and rats hid in the grass, watching as he passed. Chris got back to his blockhouse and sat down again on the beach.

The days passed slowly and uncounted. When he got hungry, he went over to the mainland one night and bought himself chips. He walked a long way along the beach and up a road. By the time he started back, it was dark. He reached the beach and walked along the sand. The tide had come in now, and it was too late for him to get back to the island until the next low tide. He continued walking along the dark beach. There seemed to be a light in front of him, a fire or something. He walked on toward the light. There were three boys about his own age, seated around a fire. He talked to them for a while and said he was waiting for the tide to go out. They offered him canned beer and asked him if he wanted to wait with them around the fire. Chris sat down gratefully.

"You're not waiting for the tide too, are ya?"

"No. We just came down here to have a drink and get ourselves warm." The boy's accent was English, but the other two were Scots.

The English boy's name was Ray, and one of the others was called Tich.

"Hey, you know something? You look just like Chris Plater when ya sit like that. Ya look a bit like Dylan, too."

"Yeah, but Dylan's got a thinner face. Chris Plater's got darker hair."

They all nodded. "It's funny, though. You look just like him."

"I heard he was in hospital," Tich said.

"Yeah, he thinks too hard, man. I reckon he needs to take a rest, or he's gonna kill himself."

Tich said, "How can he take a rest? He's what he is. He can't never change that. He's locked up in his own mind, like everyone else. For better, for worse, just like a bloody marriage."

Chris laughed. "It ain't a very nice mind to be locked up in, either," he said.

When he started back toward the island, it was just gone three o'clock in the morning. The water had just subsided below the pipeline, and some of the larger waves still washed across it, almost sweeping him away out to sea. In the middle of the pipeline the water was too deep, and he had to stand still for a while, the water washing over his boots, as he waited for the tide. His head felt heavy suddenly. He looked out across the dark sea. As far as he could see, there was nothing but gray water. He stood there, balancing against the pull of the waves as they swept over his feet. Suddenly he looked around to his right. He saw the reflection of lights on the water, oranges and reds, yellows and greens.

He stared for a moment at the reflections. They seemed to be shimmering on the water, almost moving. It seemed to him at that moment that it was like the monster of his dream coming toward him from out of the water. The oranges and the greens merged together. The reds and the yellows seemed to form an outline, a solid, real shape. The vision swept toward him. Suddenly it was more than just the shapes formed by the lights. It was a real, a palpable thing, with life, movement, of its own. It seemed just as he had always seen it, solid and yet formless.

Chris' whole body seemed to shake. The waves swept against his feet, trying to wash him away, westward toward the monster. The monster was real. It existed. The epitome of evil, a plague. He had known it. Even in the daylight, sitting in some café, drinking coffee, smoking, talking to somebody and joking about his dreams, he had always known it. His eyes held an expression of fear, of panic, of complete terror. He wanted to speak, but he couldn't. Voices seemed to echo in his ears—a low muttering, words that he

couldn't distinguish, phrases that he couldn't understand. He looked around him. There was no one there.
The pupils of his eyes seemed to dilate until they domi-
nated the whole of his face. He felt estranged suddenly
from everything. The feeling of great aloneness came
upon him mingled with his fear. He could remember nothing anymore, forgot even who he was. He
struggled to keep his balance on the narrow pipeline.
In front of him the cement seemed to have crumbled
away, and the water was deeper. He took a step forward, and his foot sank down, soaking his ankle. He
stepped back quickly. He could feel the vision on
the water, mocking him. A wave of blackness swept
before his brain. He felt as if he were about to pass out,
and he closed his eyes and opened them again quickly.
Glancing around him again, everything was black. The
waters were gray, bleak. Everything was black, everything but the lights. He felt them coming nearer to
him, the lights, the monster. It was a nightmare, but
a nightmare which was not a dream but reality. He saw
the vision of the thing in his brain. He wanted to turn
toward it, but he couldn't. The island loomed before
him, stationary, motionless. The wave of unconsciousness, of blackness, seemed to sweep across his brain.
The water below him gnawed at his feet. He felt terror, aloneness. The fear prompted him onward, and he
began to edge forward again, through the waves. He
slipped on the cracked pipeline and fought to save him-

self from falling. He managed to steady himself and looked down as he did so at the deep water on either side.

In his mind he could see the picture of himself, watch his own actions as if he were some independent on-looker. He shouted suddenly at the top of his voice, "There is no one else in the world. No other creature exists. There is no one. No one." It was as if the voice was alien to him. He started at the sound of it. "The voice does not exist. There is nothing. The voice does not understand, and so it is dead. God does not understand, and so He does not exist. The monster understands, and so it is the monster. I understand, and so I am the enemy. The waves understand, and so they are me." The fear overcame him. He moved on, almost running. His parka flapped around his sides, one moment flowing out behind him, the next moment enveloping him. He talked to himself all the time that he walked. They were the words of his mind spilling out from his lips, not speech at all, but thoughts.

Twice he slipped and almost fell. The water swept over his ankles and over the edges of his jeans. He reached the causeway at the end of the pipe-line and slipped through the seaweed and mussels onto the rocks. He stood, breathing heavily, and looked back to the sea. The lights and the reflections were gone. He jumped through the rocks and around to the beach. He stumbled on something and rested against a rock.

The wood on the beach cracked, as he moved, under his feet. He picked up some of the wood, gathered it together and tried to set it alight. The wood didn't light, and he gathered up some straw and lit that. The wind blew in from the sea and blew out his match. He tried again, sheltered the smoldering straw with his parka, and watched as it began to catch light. He threw on some of the smaller pieces of wood, then the larger ones, and stood up over the small fire. He began to speak to himself again. He talked constantly as he tended to the fire. The wind seemed to howl, drowning the crackling noises of the fire joining with the sea to form a background against his talking. The words came out sometimes half said; the sentences were half finished or seemed to make no sense.

He walked three times in a circle around the fire. His hair hung across his face; when the light of the fire caught them, his eyes gleamed slightly, as if he were drugged. The biting wind seemed not to affect him. He sat astride a rock in front of the fire, tossing wood onto it as the flames gathered strength. He felt completely uninhibited, completely free. There were no thoughts in his mind at all. He had a feeling of purpose, the knowledge that he had nothing to do, nothing else in his mind other than to exist.

He stood up again and walked to the edge of the sea. Suddenly he spoke again. He said, "The sea is mad." He looked on it compassionately. "The island is my empire." He didn't look at the island, but up at the sky. "The huts in the forest are the emperor's court. The blockhouse on the rocks is the winter palace. Life is an imperial dream, and truth is an imperial lie with the emperor as an imperial con man and his subjects as men with no eyes." He smiled, and the strength seemed to drain from his legs so that he had to move back again and sit down. "The island is an uneaten sausage which has gone moldy and been thrown away. The boy who sits on the island is a hungry fly, and the skies are the lid of a dustbin. God is the tramp who searches through the dustbin for old clothes. But one day the tramp masturbates into the dustbin and so creates the monster, which is a god, too." He looked down at his hands and held them out before the fire. The smoke from the fire blew into his face, and he turned away. When the wind shifted, he turned back. He rubbed his eyes and ran his hands around his face as if exploring it for the first time. His fear on the pipeline had completely disappeared. It was as if the incident were forgotten, vanished from his mind.

Softly he started to talk again, addressing himself to the flames. The words were so soft that they were unintelligible. The flames flickered and died slightly as he threw on more wood. He edged forward on the rock to move closer to the warmth. The corner of his parka fell across one of the smoldering logs, and he watched it as it began to burn. A small area of black appeared on the green cloth. The blackness spread, turning into a small hole, red and yellow around the edges. He watched it still, completely uninterested. Eventually the cloth broke out into a flame. He pulled it away from the fire and trod out the flame in the sand. "The flame is an opium whose effect is insanity and spreads at night to illustrate its own illumination. Tomorrow is a fire which burns in men's hearts to convince the dead that they are alive and the alive that they are dead. And words are just toys which are manipulated by mathematicians until they make sense." He stood up again and walked away, leaving the fire to burn for a while. He spent the whole night walking on the beach. Soon the fire was nothing but dead ashes. He felt no sense of time at all, and the hours passed.

He stood among the rocks and watched the sky beyond the blockhouse. Gradually a haze of red and yellow appeared on the skyline and illuminated part of the sky. He stood without moving, his eyes on the sky. The light fascinated him, almost mesmerized him. His eyes had a light of innocence in them. The effect of the haze hung in the sky, and he stood there in a trance. Slowly the sun began to rise higher against the rocks. Rays of the dawn sun spread out their long shadows weakly on the beach. Chris watched until the sun had risen over the horizon and then climbed the shaded rocks slowly up to the blockhouse and went to sleep.

VIII

During the next few days Chris stayed, sleeping and talking, on the island. He salvaged cardboard boxes and driftwood from the beach and took them up to the blockhouse with him to wedge against the large open windows in order to keep out drafts. He found an old wooden door in one of the other blockhouses, carried it back to the south end of the island, and used it to cover the opening of the large drafty room in which he had been sleeping. At night the wind was strong and rattled the wood and boxes wedged into the windows, and by day the room was dark, and he would sit in it for hours, staring at the invisible walls.

He fell into the habit of climbing every day onto the roof of the blockhouse and sitting there, watching the pipeline as it rose up from out of the sea, and the small boats as they sailed across the firth. He hadn't eaten since the last time he'd crossed the pipeline. It was days since then, and yet he didn't seem to notice it. He felt hardly any pangs of hunger at all. His clothes and his hands grew filthy. The beginnings of a beard grew on his face. Above his mouth he grew a thin Michael Chaplin moustache, and below his long matted hair his eyes looked out on the overgrown island as if permanently drugged.

No other holidaymakers came out to see him on the small island. The Scots girl he'd talked to before never returned. During the afternoon the children from the village would come out onto the pipeline to fish, but none of them approached the rocks of the island. Chris sat there alone. On the second day after he'd come back across the pipeline, he was sitting, late in the afternoon, on top of the blockhouse. The wind was cold, blowing straight through him, and he sat huddled there, his feet hanging over the edge of the blockhouse. He lit himself a cigarette. It was the first cigarette he'd smoked in three days. For a moment his head seemed to be spinning, reeling. The cigarette made him feel weak, made his head ache. He thought for a moment that he was going to fall. The whole of the landscape looked suddenly marvelous to him. He wanted to sing or speak or shout. The sea seemed to glimmer and glisten beneath the yellow sun. The sun blazed in the sky. It seemed as if it were alive. It seemed to him almost for the first time that it was a real moving thing rather than just a permanent unnoticed object hanging in the sky. As he looked at it, it was like a prolonged moment of insight, of truth. It seemed to him that the sudden truths he'd seen would not vanish as soon as his mind was about to grasp them, would not disappear like the moments of insight at sexual orgasm or like the "peak experiences" of Maslow, but were permanent, unforgettable. He found himself completely at peace, completely happy. Everything around him seemed to burn with life. The excitement of it seemed to be almost painful. He lay back on the concrete blockhouse roof, his eyes on the sky.

His eyes communicated great intensity, like the red eyes of Bardino. The whole of his expression seemed to be concentrated into his eyes. It was as if, for the first time, he saw things in their right perspective. The sun, the sea, the outline of trees and houses over on the mainland, all of them were suddenly more than just normal everyday objects to him. Suddenly he saw things as being important and alive.

For the next two days it was as if he were in a dream, deeper even in his dream than he had been on the night he crossed the pipeline. The feeling of aliveness seemed to remain with him. He wandered quite aimlessly about the island. On the second day he sat on the beach as the tide subsided below the pipeline. He watched the kids with their fishing rods as they advanced along the pipeline, shouting and arguing. Among them all there walked a girl. She was about nineteen. She had come from a car or van parked on the mainland at the beginning of the pipeline. He watched her as she picked her way along the pipeline, reached the causeway and then waded through the puddles and seaweed left by the tide until she reached the rocks. The girl wore jeans and a leather jacket. He pulled his parka around him a little tighter. The sun dazzled him, and he stared vacantly at the approaching girl.

The girl came slowly over the rocks. She seemed

to be coming toward him, slowly, unsure. She came up to where Chris was sitting, on one of the rocks. Chris watched her still. A strange feeling came over him. He wondered what she was going to do, what she wanted, who she was. She stopped in front of him. She said, "Hello, Chris."

He seemed to jump at the mention of his own name. It seemed to him that he hadn't heard the name for weeks. He had almost forgotten it. For some reason he felt scared suddenly. He didn't say anything.

Lorraine came nearer to him. She put her hand on his shoulder. She said, "D'you recognize me, Chris?"

He moved away instinctively from her, but the hand remained on his shoulder. The hand stirred something in him. He felt for a moment that possibly he knew her, and then the feeling was lost.

Lorraine sat on the rock opposite him. The sight of him as he sat there, unshaven, filthy, unable to recognize her, looking like a small child, made her feel that she wanted to cry, take hold of him and get through to him somehow, tell him who he was, who she was, what had been happening to him.

She said, "I'm Lorraine, Chris. I'm your friend."

"I know." His eyes looked at her, wild and blue, childlike and yet somehow serious and remote. She felt just as she'd often felt about him before, that somehow he saw more, realized more, understood more of what was going on around him than anyone else she knew.

He didn't say anything else. He just kept looking at her as if he were trying to place her.

She said, "I came up with Spud. He's sitting in the van. We've come to take you home, Chris."

"Who's Spud?" He didn't seem to understand, didn't seem to know what she was talking about. "I haven't got no home. I live here. I know you somehow, and yet I don't know who you are. Who are you? Why'd you come here?"

"I'm Lorraine." She pushed her hand back through her hair. She didn't seem to be able to talk to him, didn't seem to be able to make him understand her. She said, "Chris, you're not well."

"No one's well. The world's death. Everyone here must be dying, otherwise they wouldn't be here."

"But you're sick, Chris, you're ill. You don't know what you're doing, you don't know what you're saying. You need help. I've come to take you home."

He just looked at her and then out to sea. She took out her cigarettes and gave him one. He leaned forward to light it from her match, and then he looked back to the sea. He held the cigarette in front of him and seemed to be watching it, staring at it. His face was expressionless, and yet he seemed to be straining to understand her, straining to understand what she was talking about.

"We want to take you back to London. You've got to see the doctor again, Chris. We've been worrying

238

about you. Spud went to look for you down in Brighton. Then we thought you'd be up here. We've got the van on the other side of that pipeline. Spud's bought some wine." She trailed off. She didn't know what else to say. He didn't seem even to be listening to her. His mind seemed a thousand miles away, remote and unattainable.

He said suddenly, "Why do you want me to go to London?"

"Because you're ill. You're—you're sick, not well. You've got to see a doctor, Chris." She was going to say, "You're mad, around the bend," but she remained silent.

"You think I'm off my head," he said. He laughed, and then he stopped laughing and looked back around at her. "I'm not mad," he said. "I think I knew you once, a long time ago. But I don't remember you anymore. I don't know you. I can't . . . remember you. I don't wanna go to London with you. I don't wanna do anything. I wanna stay here. I don't know any of the people you know. I don't know anyone."

Lorraine drew on her cigarette. She was breathing heavily, listening to him. She looked at him. He seemed mad, and yet there was a sort of sanity about him. He was so quiet, so strange. She felt incapable of understanding him, incapable of understanding what was going on.

She said, "Look, Chris, you've been here for weeks.

Everyone's worried about you. You seem so different. When you got out of hospital, you seemed all right again, but now you seem different. While you've been here, you seem to have changed."

"Hospital?" There was a long pause. He said, "I seem to remember. . . . I had to stay in bed. . . . I wanted to get away. I wanted to come up here, and I—" He looked at her. He remembered something. He didn't know what it was. It was as if there were something in his subconscious, something trying to break through, something that he couldn't quite grasp. He struggled to try to understand it, and then suddenly it was as if he'd lost track of it altogether, as if he'd even forgotten that he was trying to remember something. He said, "Come and see the other side of the island." He got up happily, talking to her as if he were talking to himself.

They walked to the other side of the island, Lorraine merely following him. She didn't hold his hand, didn't even try to walk next to him, just followed a few feet behind. He stood on the rocks, looking down at the sea and just talking. "Sometimes I feel that coming here is somehow special. A girl came here once. I sat on the beach and talked to her." His voice trailed off for a moment. "It seems a long time ago—I don't know how long. In the end she had to go away. I thought she might come back. I waited for her for a little while. I wanted to bring her up here, show her the sea down there. Look at it. The sea is . . ." He didn't seem to be able to find the words. He turned around to her as if he'd forgotten that he'd even been speaking. He seemed to have remembered what he'd been trying to say before. He said, "I was in love with a girl called Lorraine, wasn't I? I remember things. . . . I was living with you in London. And then I came here. . . . I can't—I can't remember everything. I went to London with you on a train one night, and when we got there, there was someone else. We all got drunk . . . and Napoleon . . . Napoleon is in prison. I . . ." He stopped talking.

She put her arms around him, "Oh, Chris."

"I once wanted to kill myself here," he said. "I looked at the rocks. It was—in the past. A long time ago, before I came here this time. I looked down at the rocks, and I wanted to kill myself, but I knew if I tried, I wouldn't have been able to do it. I wasn't scared. I just knew I wouldn't be able to do it. It wouldn't have worked because the rocks aren't high enough. The rocks couldn't kill anybody. Look at them, Lorraine. Lorraine, I'm not mad. People might think I am. But I'm not mad. I've seen things. I've had . . . visions. But that's not madness. I could never go mad now. I've beaten it. I've managed not to go mad. I can't explain it. I've seen the thing I've been looking for all this time, and yet I don't seem to be able to tell anyone about it. All I know is, I'm . . . different. If I hadn't found it, then I would have gone insane, but I'm not. Or at least—I don't know what I'm saying. Perhaps I am mad. Perhaps this is what madness is. But I don't feel mad. I don't feel as if—" He just looked at her as she stood there, away from him, her hands still resting on his shoulders. "I remember there's a song. Sometimes it keeps going around and around in my brain. I remember I used to sing it. There used to be lots of people. I used to sing it to them, and it was about me. I always think, when I have it in my mind now, that it's about me. It's about . . . finding something. I used to sing it almost all the time. People used to sit and listen to it. And no one knew what it meant, even the person who wrote it. I don't think even he knew what it meant, or not completely. I used to wonder about it. I think . . . the person who wrote it . . . I think I used to know him. Perhaps he did know what it meant. I'm not sure. I know that it applied to me. I know that I used to argue with people about it and try to explain to them what it was about. And I used to write songs of my own, too, to try to explain things. But now, the thing that I was searching for when I was singing that song, I think that I've found it. I think that if I hadn't found it, it would have made me insane. And now that I have found it, perhaps I'm insane anyway." He'd finished talking, and his eyes strayed back to the sea. Lorraine noticed the gleam, the look of excitement, in them. His hair blew against his neck and his ears. She felt that she wanted to take hold of him, kiss him, pretend that he was still the same person that he'd been before, walk with him along some crowded street, fall asleep with him in some drafty alleyway. She watched his face as she lit herself another cigarette.

She said, "Come back to London with me, Chris."

"D'you think it'd be the same? Perhaps it only works here. Perhaps this feeling I get . . . it doesn't last. What if I get to London and I don't remember it any-more? I wouldn't be able to see things. I wouldn't be able to come and stand on the rocks, and—" Slowly he bent down and sat on his heels on the grass on top of the rocks. He lowered his voice until it was almost a whisper. "It's lovely here," he said. He sat looking out over the barren sea, watching the rocks and the sands and the receding waves. Madly his eyes moved over the grass in front of him and then the blue-gray land-scape out ahead.

"All right," he said. "Let me sit here for a little while first, and then I'll come with you." He turned away suddenly from the sea in front of him. "It all ends in tears anyway."

5. / *Where Emperors Stood*

LORRAINE sat in the doctor's outer office. The room was deserted. She looked around her. It reminded her of a prison, a gray, sterilized prison. She counted the number of windows, measured with her eyes the length and height of the room. Her legs were crossed in front of her. She wore a pink skirt, very short, with dark, seamless stockings. Her cigarette end burned absently in her hand. Her hair flopped forward, unattended, across her face. She had Chris' book next to her on the other chair, *A Drum for Dave Moselle*.

The book had been published just three weeks ago. Lorraine glanced down at it, at the picture of Chris standing on the front cover. She looked at the expression on his face, the expression of deepness, the expression which said, "Look, man, today I'm busy. If you've got problems, come back tomorrow sometime. Today I'm working out my own salvation." She looked at the ring he wore on his finger, the ring he had bought once on the promenade at Southend. It had cost him two and six, and he had been so hard up that Lorraine had had to lend him the money to buy it. From that day it was known as Lorraine's ring. When he didn't wear it, he carried it around with him always in his jacket pocket.

Lorraine's eyes began to grow wet as she looked down onto the cover of the book. The memories flashed into her mind. All the songs, the poems, that he had once written specially for her. All the things that she had written for him. He'd told her once that they'd brought tears to his eyes. She sat there, almost crying. She looked over at the frosted glass door leading to the next room. A dark, unrecognizable figure moved about behind the glass. She listened, trying to catch what was being said, but she could hear nothing. Everything was silent still. Her mind went blank again, all the memories lost. But there had been other things to remember too. Calella de la Costa, in Spain. The first time they ever went there in the days when they owned the world and every other gesture was a laugh and every other thought was of a soggy Durex left strewn on the roadside somewhere in sticky Spain. She smiled to herself. There were lots of things behind them, lots of things in the past. Time passed quickly, frighteningly. What was going to happen in the future? That was what mattered. That was what mattered.

She looked up at the door again and then down at her cigarette. The cigarette had almost burned away. She lit another one and sat smoking it in silence until the frosted glass door finally opened. The doctor came into the room and closed the door. Doctor Stevenson took off his glasses and rubbed his eyes. He replaced his glasses and sat down behind his desk.

Lorraine watched him. His charcoal-gray suit was immaculate; his shirt was spotless. He arranged himself behind the desk and smiled his tired, warm-seeming smile. He said to Lorraine, "I'd like to know if Chris has any relations."

She nodded. "Yeah, I think he has. He doesn't see anything of them anymore. In Hertfordshire somewhere. Why, d'you need to know?"

Stevenson stood up again and walked over to her. He stood looking down at her, his hand on her shoulder. Then he sat down by her side. She could see that he had been sweating. The sweat stuck out on his forehead and around the tight collar of his shirt. He said, "His nearest relations have to be informed by law of his medical state." He lowered his voice fractionally. "But personally I think the first person to be told should be you." He looked at her directly.

Lorraine said, "Told what?"

He comforted her, his hand gently around her shoulder. "My dear, as far as it is possible for our society to judge, Christopher Plater is incurably insane."

II

A large group of girls stood chanting and singing outside the wrought-iron gates.

On the ground the frost retreated slowly as the October sun arched its way over the large, foreboding group of buildings. One of the girls held a placard: CHRIS PLATER IS SANE. They stood by the gates and pressed up hard against the brick walls, the buildings hardly visible to them through the palisade of leafless trees.

The van drew up and had to stop about twenty yards from the group of girls. The three of them got out, and Spud walked in the middle, one hand on Carol, one on Lorraine. A girl stopped them and gave them a letter to give to Chris. The sound of the singing followed them, noisy and uncontrolled, along the drive between the trees. Carol dropped her menthol cigarette amid the decaying leaves, and they walked on.

As they walked along the corridors, the insane chatter of the wards and of the single rooms came to them and passed. At the far room the noises of the asylum passed behind them. The male nurse opened the door and stood back. Chris sat at the window on the far side of the room. He turned to them slowly without recognition. Lorraine went forward to him quickly and took his hand. He made no movement but just looked at her vacantly. She bit back her tears and released him.

Spud said, "We got some cigarettes, Chris."

"Cigarettes?"

Spud took out the cigarette packet and walked over toward the barred window.

Chris took one. There was a great, overcoming air of sadness about him. He put it to his mouth, and Spud lit it. There was silence again. The only sound in the whole room was that of the chanting from the girls just visible from the window, standing at the gate.

The whole interview passed in the same way. They were all strangers. Time passed slowly, and Carol stood with Spud, both of them helpless, as Lorraine tried to talk.

Carol caught Spud's eye, and the helplessness they both felt communicated itself between them. Spud and Carol said good-bye, and they both left to wait outside.

Lorraine stood with Chris at the window. He was silent still as his eyes passed over the group of girls standing at the gate. She watched him in all his dignity as he stood there.

"Are you really mad, Chris?"

"What is madness?"

She put her hand on his shoulder, and then suddenly

she couldn't help herself. She pulled tight against him, buried her head against his chest. "Oh, Christ." She was crying, and it altered her voice, made her falter and made the words, when they came, come out in a rush. "Oh, I wish you could come back with me, Chris. I wish I could suddenly wake up and find that none of this had ever happened." She cried without being able to stop.

Chris pulled her away from him so that they could look into each other's faces. Lorraine checked herself. She looked deep into the sadness of his eyes, but all she could see was the expression of sadness and thoughtfulness that had been there so often before.

As she watched, in the corner of one eye she saw the flickering of a tear. When he spoke she felt suddenly scared, as if he were talking to her from the dead. "I'm in my paradise, Lorraine, can't you see that? I've beaten it, Lorraine. I've found my paradise. This is it. This room." His voice was softer and slower than anything she had ever heard.

She put her hands to her eyes. He held her briefly, and then he turned away again to the window. Before he turned away, he said, "I wish you could be in my paradise with me, Lorraine. I wish you could be here with me."

He stood at the window as she left the room, the moisture gathering in his eyes. He looked through the bars at the group of girls who stood by the gate, at Lorraine and Spud and Carol as they walked down the path, and yet his eyes did not see them. He listened to the sound of the singing, and yet his ears did not hear them.

Crudely, roughly, his voice laying its emphasis on all the wrong words, his eyes looking forward still and seeing only the distant horizon, he began to sing. For a moment his words mingled with those of the girls at the gate. "Hey, Mr. Tambourine Man . . ." and then his words became lost again suddenly, and inaudible.